# "You probably shouldn't kiss me again."

Bindi waited as the music disappeared into the hot silence, her breath held, her thoughts on pause, watching him. Santino took the bait, his tattooed forearms tensing as he stilled his strong fingers on the piano keys, and sent her a slow, challenging smile. Bindi moved.

She cut away the distance between them, her bare feet soundless on the marble floor as she edged between the piano and the wide, plush bench. Her legs bumped his, forcing him to release the keys and nudge the bench backward.

In front of him, she absorbed that sexy, challenging smile with one of her own, and dropped her butt onto the keyboard. The noise resonated in her ears. "Kissing me like that? Holding me like that? Going there again would be a mistake you don't want to make, Santino."

"Is it a mistake *you* want to make? Is that how you want to play this?"

Caught off guard, she stammered, "This? There is no *this*. Don't start thinking there is. What I mean is, you shouldn't figure a kiss is going to make me more inclined to help you find Al. In fact, I'm less inclined. I'm done with him, and I want to be done with you."

Santino reached for her lock pendant. With a faint tug, he pulled her forward until her mouth was close enough to sample. "Can you last an entire conversation without lying?"

"Yes." *Possibly.*

"My father's not in this house, and he's not sitting at this ⬚no. It's you and it's me, Bindi." He released her pendant, ⬚ let his hands glide freely up her thighs and tangle in ⬚ her dress. "And I don't see you walking away."

Dear Reader,

Ever want to get away? Perhaps to distance yourself from a less-than-ideal situation? Or to just see something new? Many attribute my insatiable wanderlust to personality traits and astrological characteristics. When travel isn't an option, writing is. New characters often take me away and invite me into their worlds. And sometimes we become so tight so quickly that I bring them back with me.

Which is why *Mine Tonight* is Bindi Paxton's story. If you read *Night Games*, then you know Bindi well. Or you *think* you do. She's waited impatiently for me to reveal who she truly is. Despite her gritty past and damaging mistakes, she's a beautiful person deserving of redemption—much like Santino Franco. Bindi and Santino can't seem to escape themselves, each other *or* what awaits them within the Blue Dynasty.

May this book take you away.

XOXO

*Lisa Marie Perry*

# *Mine* TONIGHT

Lisa Marie Perry

HARLEQUIN® KIMANI™ ROMANCE

Recycling programs
for this product may
not exist in your area.

ISBN-13: 978-0-373-86399-0

Mine Tonight

For questions and comments about the quality of this book please contact us at CustomerService@Harlequin.com.

**Printed in U.S.A.**

**Lisa Marie Perry** thinks an imagination's a terrible thing to ignore. So is a good cappuccino. After years of college, customer service gigs and a career in caregiving, she at last gave in to buying an espresso machine and writing to her imagination's desire. Lisa Marie lives in America's heartland, and she has every intention of making the Colorado mountains her new stomping grounds. She drives a truck, enjoys indie rock, collects Medieval literature, watches too many comedies, has a not-so-secret love for lace and adores rugged men with a little bit of nerd.

### Books by Lisa Marie Perry

### Harlequin Kimani Romance

*Night Games*
*Midnight Play*
*Just for Christmas Night*
*Mine Tonight*

Visit the Author Profile page at
Harlequin.com for more titles

For my babies—

Whenever I want to be wiser, funnier,
stronger or kinder, all I have to do is think of you.
I don't want a world without you in it.

# Chapter 1

"Got some info about your father's ex-fiancée. Bindi Paxton. A sexy little piece. Keep in contact with her?"

Santino Franco knew someone had followed him after he'd left the Las Vegas sports physical therapy clinic that had served as his haven for the past two years. A male in heavy-soled footwear. Combat boots, maybe. Photographer? Reporter? A genuine threat?

Tonight's rehabilitation evaluation and endurance-centered training session had reset his limits, but the violent adrenaline rush had only sharpened his awareness. Pace slow, senses alert, he'd crossed casually to the parking lot with his duffel bag hooked over one shoulder and his fists hungry for permission to act.

But the name Bindi Paxton had caught him off guard, forced him to engage. Press preyed on him to feed their questions about his father, Alessandro Franco, a prominent member of the one percent who'd fallen from grace and was as of two weeks ago MIA, but this was the first time anyone had used Alessandro's ex-fiancée as a tactic.

"There're two ways we can end this game," he threatened when his tracker remained camouflaged in the shadows offered by the lazy February sunset. "You back off, or I make you back off."

"Wouldn't mind the challenge, 'cept the .38 wound in

my shoulder burns like a mother." The stranger stepped into the periphery of a floodlight beam. Tall and dark, his accent and features suggested Middle Eastern descent.

Instinct told Santino to tread on—carefully. "You a fed? Military?"

"A jack of a few decent trades. A problem solver, really. Heard you wanted to find your father. I don't have a badge or nice, neat paperwork. But I'm as legit as they come. Name's Zaf. Know where Bindi is?"

"If you want to find Bindi, Zaf, try looking behind a few whiskey sours or under any of Vegas's geriatric millionaires." Venomous words, but they didn't spare him the images of Bindi that the phrase "sexy little piece" evoked.

She *was* sexy. He'd believed it every second of every day he'd shared space with her in the Francos' Lake Las Vegas mansion. She had a secretive smile, midnight-radio voice and clothes that were figure-hugging enough to distract even a man whose life now consisted of used-to-bes and could've-beens.

Struggling with the aftereffects of an injury that had cost him his NFL career—professionals called it post-traumatic stress; he called it hell—he'd used animosity and hostility to fight all the ways she enticed him. And he'd fixated on protecting his family's interests from her, a serial gold digger who'd worn deceit like a favorite dress, who'd used herself as a commodity, who'd held every intention of becoming his father's fourth wife.

"About Bindi." Zaf unzipped his jacket to drag a thick envelope from an interior pocket. Pain distorted his expression at the choppy movement. When Santino glanced down he saw a holstered Glock nestled against his side. "She's not in Las Vegas."

"She's gone?"

Just like his father. Alessandro Franco had been missing for fifteen days, escaping federal charges and an NFL investigation of misconduct during his reign as owner of the city's professional football franchise, the Las Vegas Slayers. He'd vanished as though he were a ribbon of smoke uncurling into the air of a crowded club.

What did it mean that Bindi, who'd lost access to certain connections and protections when his father had ended their engagement months ago, was now missing?

"Concerned about her?" Zaf's voice was neutral.

"A woman disappearing in this city's a damn good cause for concern, don't you think?" Especially if she might have been connected to his father's illegal activities. Perhaps there had been more to their relationship than he'd thought.

Zaf remained silent, reactionless.

"She's an ex-congressman's kid. Why isn't her family all over national news?"

"Let's say Mommy and Daddy have no comment when it comes to their only offspring. The elite Paxtons of Illinois don't invite that one home for Sunday dinners. Besides, I know where she is."

"Where?" Santino hoped he didn't sound like he cared too much.

"She booked a flight out of McCarran International last week. If she's downing whiskey or searching for a new sugar daddy, she's doing it on the Seychelles."

"She left the country?"

"She got scoped, same as everybody else the feds singled out for a closer look. They figure her hands are clean enough for her to travel. But I'm getting this feeling that when Al comes up for air, he might go straight to her."

There was no way in hell his father would come to his sons, that was for sure. "He treated her horribly. Dumped her."

"Money can make some women forgiving. With Franco money, Bindi might be *very* forgiving."

*She deserves better than that.*

Not that Santino could identify *better* or had any right to decide what his father's ex did or didn't deserve, but when it came to being used and dropped, he and Bindi Paxton shared a few scars.

There was a vulnerability about her that common sense warned him to resist. Still, the grand Franco mansion had made for close quarters, and yeah, there'd been moments when common sense had left him hanging.

A moment when he'd walked in on her fixing gourmet s'mores in the middle of the night, and she'd offered him a timid smile and a s'more before charging off to her quarters. A moment when he'd caught her daydreaming at a gala and for a split second figured it hadn't mattered to him whether she was bored or designing her next scheme—she was so damn beautiful. A moment when he'd found her shuddering with tears in her eyes and he'd wanted to hurt Alessandro for wrecking her.

She'd tempted him to cross lines that shouldn't be crossed. She was out of his reach now, and he couldn't let himself miss her magnetism enough to change that.

"How'd you get her whereabouts?"

"Intel," Zaf replied, tucking the envelope under an arm and awkwardly lighting a cigarette. "My contacts can report back to me anything from the VIN of the convertible she rented on Cora Island to what she packed in her fancy purple luggage."

"Convertible? Purple luggage?" It sounded as though Zaf was outright stalking Bindi. Probably had been keeping tags on him, too. What game was Zaf playing and for whom? If Zaf could find his father, then he was game to play along until he could figure out what was going on.

"Collecting details is just part of my job." Zaf exhaled a stream of smoke from the shadows before pitching the cigarette to the ground and snuffing it under a boot. "Quitting. It's a process."

Santino ignored the wry aside. "So that's all you have? Bindi's on the Seychelles?"

"Those are the highlights. There's more—a hell of a lot more—in this file. But first, why don't you tell me how she'd get herself set up on some island, in a villa that has a six-month reservation wait list?"

Six months ago, it'd been August. Alessandro had broken up with Bindi in August. Chances were he hadn't given her some island getaway as a parting gift, so the villa must've been booked while things were still good between them, when he might've cared about impressing her.

Realization dawned. It was February. Almost Valentine's Day, one of many holidays that hadn't mattered to him since his girlfriend had traded him for a rookie New England Patriot.

Vaguely he recalled Bindi bragging to the sugar-baby socialites she'd run with in Las Vegas that her fiancé had given her carte blanche to plan a Valentine's vacation.

He'd assumed everything between them had ended with their engagement.

"I remember her planning a trip," he told Zaf. "My father ate the cost."

"A honeymoon?"

"Naw—she had ideas about taking a cruise around the world. The island could've been for a number of reasons. Could've been something my father threw out there to distract her."

"Damn expensive distraction. Is that why Al told her to step? Upkeep not worth it?"

"Might be part of it." A bigger part probably had more to do with his father's compulsion to screw over the people he said he cared about.

But Santino hadn't wanted to dwell on that negativity. All he wanted was to concentrate on rehab, on his quiet mission to regain control of the career he'd lost. Chasing a comeback that the more pessimistic of his doctors and athletic trainers insisted would be a miracle that'd defy the laws of science or would be the false hope that might get him onto the field but would likely lead to paralysis, he thought he'd get a reprieve from federal investigators, blood-lusting media, his own urge to hunt Alessandro and drag him home to justice that'd be neither clean nor forgiving.

For the umpteenth time since he'd been introduced to the phrase *incomplete spinal cord injury*, he cursed the tackle that had turned him into a walking dead man.

A Las Vegas Slayers defensive lineman had targeted him two seasons ago, taking him out of the game with an illegal hit—a hit ordered by the man who'd owned the team then.

Alessandro Franco.

It had been a bounty, a call his father had made to fix the game and manipulate a gambling ring.

While Alessandro was running from the repercussions of his crimes, Santino was left to pick up every microscopic piece of his shattered life.

He'd lost more than his place on the Cardinals' roster and in the NFL. He'd become a prisoner to rehab and revenge, and fear sometimes suggested he was so psychologically jarred that he'd never recover.

"Bindi Paxton's the means," Zaf said rationally, "but finding Alessandro Franco is the end."

"Alive. I want him found alive."

"Of course." A flash of white teeth shone in the shadows. "I'd rather see a mouse crawl in a cage than crush its neck in a trap."

Santino frowned. "No results, no cash."

"Consider this a good deed. Pro bono."

"What's your stake in it?"

"Bringing Alessandro in will look nice on my record. My record needs, uh, redemption, you could say."

"Zaf—what's your full name?"

"Just Zaf is all you need to know."

"Yeah? Well, I don't trust you."

"Trust is more hassle than it's worth. Who can anyone trust? Family? Your father sold you out for some sports bets—can you trust him?"

Santino would always love his father. It was a deathbed promise he'd made to his mother. He still honored him, because the "dutiful son" part of him just wouldn't die. But he'd never trust the man again. It stung like a bitch that this was reality.

"Or your godfather, Gian DiGorgio?" Zaf persisted. "Can you trust him?"

Gian, who ran one of the most exclusive casinos in the country, was Alessandro's oldest friend and was facing convictions for his alleged facilitation of the gambling ring. "What do you know about Gian?"

"The security at his casino is lax. DiGorgio's cameras have blind spots, his boys have slow reflexes and the system's firewalls are laughable."

"You've been getting acquainted with his security systems?"

"Research."

Unease crawled up Santino's spine. "How do I know you're not one of DiGorgio's boys?"

"Huh—guess you don't. But think about this. Gian

DiGorgio's playing with a trick deck. He's got the brains and the balls to rig his casino with bad security. That's strategy. He's smart. He's a liar. And I can guaran-damn-tee his next step is recommending you a PI to find Alessandro. Just to prove he's one of the good guys."

Gian was a skilled betrayer. That wasn't news to Santino. But he didn't trust Zaf any more than he trusted his godfather.

Zaf shrugged a shoulder. "Let's talk about your brother. More specifically, his tasty bedmate, Charlotte Blue. She's more involved in your troubles than you probably think."

Wasn't it friggin' funny how the name Blue kept resurfacing as his world splintered to pieces?

When Alessandro had architected claims that Charlotte's father, Marshall Blue, had coerced Alessandro to sell the Las Vegas Slayers franchise to him over a year ago, Santino had reacted with vengeance. He'd been the heir apparent, next in line to own the team. The Blues were building a dynasty from *his* legacy. And he'd single-mindedly wanted to destroy it.

That was before the truth had come down as cold and sharp as a guillotine's blade.

"Charlotte's got a friend in DEA. Josephine de la Peña," Zaf said. "She followed a few bread crumbs, found out your father had made some suspect moves. Which led to the dirt she's got on your godfather. Did you know that?"

"No." He'd known that the feds were hunting. He *hadn't* known that the woman his brother was currently sleeping with had a friend leading the hunt.

"Gian DiGorgio knows." Zaf turned the envelope in his hands. "Want to get to Bindi Paxton? Want this file to make it easier? Agree to do what's necessary to draw out Alessandro, then deliver him to me. I'll turn him over to the feds—alive *and* unharmed."

It took Santino a split second to make his decision. "Give me the file."

On nights like tonight, when he couldn't shake off the shadows, Santino stayed awake straight through, idly praying for the kind of exhaustion that'd force him to surrender to sleep.

With a file dedicated to Bindi Paxton along with a contact number for Zaf in his possession, and a mood blacker than the paint on his truck, he got behind the wheel and figured if he couldn't escape the shadows, he'd confront them.

Not yet through with the city, Santino rejected the impulse to storm his father's Lake Las Vegas estate. Eventually he might. For a while the place had been home, even if crowded with household staff and Alessandro's trophy fiancée. But with most of the staff, the trophy, Santino and Alessandro himself gone, no one occupied the multimillion-dollar mansion besides the head housekeeper, whose unbending loyalty to a betrayer of a man wouldn't set her free.

Night traffic slowed his speed, kept him on the road longer than he liked. More tourists, he figured, and it for damn certain had to do with Las Vegas being high on back-to-back sports victories. The city's homegrown pro boxer had recently beaten a Czech Republic challenger to retire undefeated, and the scandal-drenched Slayers were now Super Bowl champs.

Stress coated his nerves so thickly and tautened his muscles so violently that he was glad to hand off the truck to a DiGorgio Royal Casino valet and start walking again before the pain could start.

The cash in his gold clip he wouldn't miss, and he had access to more. His mind needed peace; his body needed satisfaction. But he hadn't come to his godfather's top-tier casino, with its Art Deco influence and no-sex escorts who were expertly skilled in tempting the clientele past their inhibitions and gambling limits, to play.

No high-stakes games. No high-class hookups. No to the woman who'd appointed herself his private concierge, who had suggestions on how to make tonight an unforgettable experience. Unfortunately, he didn't think he'd ever experience pleasure the way he had with Tabitha. His injury had taken care of that.

With Tabitha, he'd been whole. He might get back into his jersey and celebrate a miraculous comeback, but he'd never be whole again.

Besides, there was someone he was here to see. Both stoic and slick, Gian DiGorgio was a man you needed to look in the eye when you talked to him.

Reserved for celebrities seeking discretion and for the riskiest of high rollers, the casino's Titanium Club was a top-floor sinners' playground. Rarely was the owner accessible outside the club. Guests weren't allowed beyond the gold-plated doors without invitation.

Anger was Santino's invitation to invade the club. Godfather to both Santino and his younger brother, Nate, Gian owed them answers. He called himself old-fashioned, a man of simple expectations. He defined *family* as a bond borne of loyalty, protection, respect—meaning if you didn't give him all three, you weren't his family.

In the wake of his father's disappearance, Santino had come to him numerous times for answers. But Gian offered silence. It was a betrayal Santino couldn't allow and hypocrisy from a man he no longer trusted.

Because Al wasn't operating on all cylinders. To fade into nothingness while under media and federal scrutiny, he'd required the services of a trusted expert. Gian Di-Gorgio—Italian billionaire, certified genius, celebrated hedonist, worldwide playboy—possessed the cunning mind, international connections and dark influence to make it happen.

Bribery and a few cold threats didn't get Santino into the club, but the hassle brought his godfather to the corridor.

Dark-suited, silver-haired and grim-faced, Gian contrasted against the brilliant luxury around him. A devil at home in his bright, glittering and expensive hell.

*"Farsi da parte. Il ragazzo è la famiglia."*

Gian's command parted the barricade of security guarding the entrance. The personable "relax—I'm on *your* side" smile Gian offered him now was one Santino had never trusted. Gian smiled that smile before he knifed associates, friends, lovers and even blood family in their backs. It was the smile he wore for cameras and investigators in his portrayal of a cooperative suspect.

"You want in? *Dai*," Gian said, regarding his godson with suspicion before escorting him into the Titanium Club. "I wasn't expecting you."

"Always expect family." A-list guests no longer crowded the gemstone-pebbled carpet. Eager gamblers no longer competed for space at the polished table games. The bar had too many vacant seats. The air was too fragrant—no, too clean—for the peak of night.

Where were the smokers, the drinkers, the hard-partying risk takers?

Avoiding connection to a place that any day might see its doors closed if Gian was more than suspected of facilitating illegal sports wagering—that was where.

"A slow night," Gian said, unconcerned. "Luck's on your side. You can have your pick of tables." He reached into the breast pocket of his jacket, removed a slim titanium case. "A cigar for your trouble at the door."

"No."

"They're King of Denmarks."

"I don't want to smoke. Or take over a table."

"Well." Gian put the case away. "This ain't the destination for you."

"Where'd you send my father?"

At the blunt question, Gian flicked an irritated glance at the smattering of guests in their vicinity then clasped Santino's shoulder. His next words were low, tense. "It was a bright day when Al and Gloria—bless her soul—asked me to be your godfather. I was honored to accept and I take my duty seriously. So I'll guide you and look out for you, *mi figlio*, but I won't tolerate disrespect."

Santino shrugged off Gian's hand. "Neither will I. How deep underground is he?"

"I'm not Al's keeper."

"I don't believe that." Gian hadn't been formally convicted, but Santino believed he was guilty. "What do you know about Bindi Paxton?"

"She's a risk," Gian said automatically, as though he'd considered this before, "and Al's better off to be done with her."

"Dad's weak. He's close to breaking. If he breaks, he talks. Without his confession on the table, you have a stronger defense."

"Enough—"

"But sending him away doesn't guarantee a free pass for you, Gian."

*"Che cazzo?"* Gian poked his index finger square in the center of Santino's forehead. "A man doesn't believe

rumors over his family's word. He doesn't accuse, convict and sentence his godfather—and his father, for that matter—without asking for the truth."

Santino knocked Gian's hand away and was tempted to let his aggression fly unrestrained. He was that weary and reckless. "A man doesn't pay someone to make sure his son rides out of a game on a cart."

"Don't infect my casino with some vendetta. Go home. Rest. Come back when you're ready to gamble and we can forget this happened." Gian studied him for a quiet moment. "Al doesn't share his plans. If he'd told me about the bounty, I would've canceled it. You'd still be on Arizona's roster and you'd still have what's-her-name in your bed."

"Tabitha."

But Gian already knew that.

"*Sì*. Tabitha. Funny. Magnificent body. You miss that, don't you?"

"Yes." Except it was more complicated than wanting Tabitha back. He didn't. Sex and good times aside, it was hard to miss a football bunny.

He missed the person *he'd* been when he'd loved her—because feeling invincible had felt so friggin' incredible. Santino had made rehabilitation an obsession. He *had* to conquer the effects of his damaged spinal cord. A thirty-eight-year-old plagued with insomnia, weak erections and random muscle spasms? He would've written himself off as a lost cause, except for the fact that somehow in the wake of hell he'd reset his body's limits to achieve strength and muscle tone that were far superior to what they'd been during his fourteen years as a tight end.

A few more active seasons should've been guaranteed. A first-round draft pick, he'd from the start considered victories as vital as oxygen. He'd deserved a chance to experience the twilight of his NFL career. Instead it'd been severed with an illegal hit that had crushed a spinal disc and could've paralyzed or killed him.

"At least ten Tabithas are in the Mahogany Lounge right now, waiting to be picked like ripe fruit off a tree," Gian offered. "There's a rough aura about you, but you've got your reasons. Let your money and good sense do the grunt work. Go downstairs. Take your pick. Let her keep you occupied."

"Occupied? So I don't show up here asking questions?"

"Next time I won't be such a pleasant guy about it, *mi figlio.*"

The parting words—and the line of Titanium Club security guards advancing on him—signaled it was his cue to walk.

A rage-fueled confrontation was a dumb-ass mistake Santino couldn't make again. Because Bindi Paxton's cooperation wouldn't be won through anger. She wasn't responsible for his pain, and he didn't want to add to hers. He'd confront her with composure, would influence her coolly, would coax her softly, if he was capable of it.

And he'd get her back to Las Vegas fast, because if he got stranded on some island where the only familiar face was one he hadn't been able to bar from his dirtiest, most honest dreams, there'd be no one to save him from himself.

## Chapter 2

No one knew her here.

Anonymity and every indulgence she could request on a pristine speck of Seychelles paradise might not be enough to make Bindi Paxton *completely* forget the crapstorm she'd made of her life in the States, but she couldn't deny it came close.

A Mahé island hideaway? Sparkling white-sand beaches that unrolled into radiant crystal waters? Hot, vibrant days and warm, teasing evening breezes? A secluded ten-thousand-euro-a-night coastline estate?

Cora Island might be considered a Silhouette wannabe—geographically smaller with appealing attractions mimicking that of the larger island—and its nightlife left something to be desired, but it was four square kilometers of preserved beauty and creole architecture.

And strangers who didn't know who she was and what she'd done.

Recent reality found her subletting a showgirl's apartment and living off the sale of her Lamborghini and what she earned hawking gossip to tabloids in Las Vegas. Packing her bags and jetting off for a prepaid vacation was one last glorious throwback to the lifestyle she'd probably never have again.

She'd come here to find what she needed: a sense of

direction. She didn't mind that people wondered why her coveted rental estate was adorned in romantic Valentine's Day glamour yet she was traveling solo.

Aside from souvenirs, selfies and a sense of peace she hadn't been able to find in Las Vegas, she intended to take no part of her island experience home to the US with her.

If not for an email reminder from the Mahé to Cora helicopter service, she might've forgotten about the vacation and Valentine's Day altogether.

*Plan the trip, Bindi. It's yours. My gift to you. By Valentine's Day, you're going to be my wife.*

Her ex-fiancé and his dead promises. Those promises plus a handcrafted engagement ring had reeled her into Alessandro Franco's world, and she'd let herself drown in illusions of marriage and the kind of stability only money and status could secure.

Then he'd lied, cheated and dropped her ass. At least she hadn't slept with him.

"To holding out," Bindi muttered into her champagne flute. Withholding sex ended a war in *Lysistrata* but hadn't earned her a prenup-free marriage. The Krug Clos d'Ambonnay sparkled silently as she drank.

Delegating her hostess duties to a perky server, she deserted her front-door post. Greeting *"Bienvenue! Viens dans!"* and passing out lock necklaces to women and key necklaces to men weren't rocket science, but got old fast.

Bindi hadn't wanted to waste Valentine's harping on how she'd let yet another man con and abuse her. Determined to spend every euro in the discretionary allowance account Alessandro had arranged for her, she'd told people at the hotel and the island's bar to save the date for a lock-and-key party at her estate, Villa Soleil.

Guests drank liquor, sampled offerings from an

aphrodisiac-themed buffet, indulged in the creamy white and rich dark streams of chocolate pouring from the golden fountain, flirted as keys twisted into locks.

Carefully snaking through the crush, Bindi felt the delicate lock pendant bounce against her in a quiet rhythm. No key had breached her lock, but perhaps the moment had come to change that.

Was she ready for this?

She had to be. Why else had she hotfooted it to Victoria for a mani-pedi and new clothes?

The mani-pedi had relaxed her. As for the clothes…

The short black lace cocktail dress, with its long sleeves, deep V in the back and clever nude silk underlayer, was the sexiest she'd wiggled into since her ex had ended their engagement. He'd had his demands—her dressing provocatively being one of them. After he'd broken up with her, she'd worn jeans, sweats and flats, anything that made her feel okay with herself.

With her fair skin strategically exposed, freshly dark-dyed hair gathered high and her burgundy fingernails gleaming under the estate's shimmering splendor, she silently repeated, "Go for it," as she zeroed in on *him*.

The small pep talk had always given her guts. Bravery. Bravado.

As Senator Roscoe Rayburn Paxton's daughter, she'd needed that.

*Unlock me, stranger.* Men in leather, Afros and piercings weren't her usual fare. Maybe it was exactly that, the differentness of him, which drew her in. Maybe she'd like him. Maybe this would be the start of something pure, and he'd introduce her to a relationship that was based on romance or heat, not business negotiations.

Wouldn't that be the ultimate way to kiss goodbye all

the lies and power plays that had conceived her hoax of an engagement?

Wouldn't that help her believe that she was changing her ways and ending the self-destructive patterns that had only hurt her in the past?

Oh, he had his eye on her. Even as he tried to turn his key in another woman's lock and doused her with the seduction of his rich creole voice, he kept Bindi in his sights.

*Name?* She didn't know. *Net worth?* She didn't care. *Married?* Oh, God, she hoped not. She would never be *that* woman again.

A bit of internet snooping could answer her questions. In her days of drifting from one society king to the next, she'd made sure to do her homework first—comparing risks to benefits. Emotions hadn't factored, until she'd lent her sympathy and trust to a Las Vegas widower in spite of the reasons she shouldn't.

Now that she'd taken herself out of the gold-digging game, she wanted a man to share something more with.

She had another week on the Seychelles, an island full of people she wouldn't mind getting to know, and a new life waiting for her back in Las Vegas that she was desperate to change for the better as soon as possible.

What happened on the island would stay on the island. On Cora she pretended to be the old her—carefree, disgustingly wealthy, confident beyond measure. Pretended she wasn't anxious, struggling and ashamed that she'd let herself hit the bottom again.

But, somehow, her spirit remained intact.

So. At least she hadn't slept with Alessandro Franco *or* let him crush her spirit.

"Cheers to that." Finishing the champagne and resolving to drink a whiskey sour next, she strode through her dreamworld party to the man who watched her.

Santino was watching her.

When he'd arrived at Villa Soleil, Cora Island's prized private coastline estate, he had been waylaid on the tea-light candlelit veranda and blasted with the noise of voices competing against crunk music. A woman in a red-smocked costume had handed him a silver necklace with a key pendant, divulged that tonight's game was all about connections and urged him to try as many locks as possible.

Screw connections. He hadn't taken off for the middle of the Indian Ocean for that. What he wanted was Bindi Paxton, alone and in the mood to help him out. If she'd had a part in his father's disappearance and decided to give Santino her loyalty, together they could draw the man out.

As for keys and locks and whatever other plans she had to squander a desperate aging man's money? Screw that, too.

But then *she* had cut into his line of vision, breasts jiggling delicately as she wound temptingly through the crowds, and he'd forgotten his motives and everything else but the demanding sensation jolting through him. A dark-haired stranger in a lace dress that barely concealed her...

*Holy...*

Curves like that didn't need lace. If she were his, if she said yes, he'd undress her. Squeeze her. Stroke her. Open her so his mouth could taste, bite and tease.

Legs like hers didn't need the accentuation of dagger heels—not when he'd rather have those taut, slender limbs propped on his shoulders or folded around his hips.

A redhead in a strapless dress appeared in front of

him, grinning in a way that made her eyes all but crinkle shut behind her black-rimmed glasses. "Swear, this feels like spring break in Cabo all over again. Um…here goes. If Sadie Hawkins can choose her guy, then I can choose the guy who puts his key in my lock." She gasped, her fingers frozen on her necklace. "That sounded obscene."

Santino might've laughed as he brought his key toward her lock, but his awareness had swung directly back to the mystery brunette as she and a few other women were drawn into a huddle of men.

What the hell was he doing? He'd come to the Seychelles to have a face-to-face with Bindi, not to stick his key into one woman's lock while tracking another who was hotter than Hades.

A click penetrated his thoughts, and he glanced down to see the lock now open. "We're a fit."

"We're not," the redhead retorted above the music, glancing over her shoulder, then at him again. She snapped the lock shut, retreating. "Obviously your attention's on a short dress."

Actually, the woman *in* it, but the point was crystal clear. "Sorry," he said. But that didn't slow her angry steps or make him feel any less like an ass.

Or persuade him to resume his search for his father's ex-fiancée. His gaze returned to that lace-covered ass, dropped to trace the quirky bow of her hyperextended legs.

*Hyperextended?* Double-jointed legs weren't exactly uncommon, but his heart panicked anyway.

Because the only woman he knew who possessed a pair of long, double-jointed pins had worn his father's ring.

Blending into the cluster circling the buffet, Santino signaled for a waiter carting around a carnal-red platter.

*"Des huîtres, monsieur?"* the waiter offered, presenting the platter. "Oysters?"

"No."

"Pomegranate? Strawberry?"

"Question."

Lowering the platter, the waiter replied, *"Si ce n'est pas sur les entrées, je ne puex pas vous aider.* I must refer you to the hostess." Peering around, he indicated the woman with the incredible backside.

The hair must've thrown him. When he'd known her, she'd had lighter, blonder hair.

And he'd never stared at her ass the way he had tonight.

*Get past that. She's here. Now get to her.*

He fixed his gaze *above* her waist—which ceased being a smart decision the second she twirled around and rewarded him a perfect view of her more-than-perfect rack.

Getting out of this house, taking the next helicopter to Mahé and returning when he could trade lust for logic was what he wanted. Problem was, he couldn't afford that kind of delay.

The longer it took to get inside Bindi's head, the crappier his chances were of establishing an alliance. He hoped he could turn her, get her on his side. He could better protect her that way.

After reading the contents of the envelope he'd taken from Zaf—a man whom he'd learned after some swift, discreet digging of his own was a military specialist last known as Archangel and whose traceable record ended several years ago—he'd determined that Bindi's life had taken a one-eighty.

The lifestyle she presented for the guests roaming the villa was false. She now lived in one of the more dangerous spots in Las Vegas and had no verifiable income source. She'd been his father's toy. Aiding him to evade his demons would downgrade her from toy to expendable pawn.

Santino refused to see that happen to her.

Still, he didn't regret being the one to show up here and prick her luxurious bubble.

"On second thought," he said to the waiter, "I need a whiskey sour sent to the hostess."

When had the house become so jam-packed? During the crunk song Bindi had danced to in a circle of expensive-suited men whose keys she'd politely rejected? She'd broken away to resume her quest for the man whose Lenny Kravitz look had caught her interest earlier, but where was he?

She stopped to regroup. A gray-haired, sun-darkened waiter penetrated the crowd, greeting her as *madame* and proffering a glass.

Was he psychic? The fabulous concierge at the island's resort hotel had highly recommended him and the other servers for this special occasion, but Professor X–style mind reading was a skill the woman hadn't mentioned.

Mesmerized, Bindi accepted the drink. Admiring the flawlessly sliced orange wheel and plump cherry, she recognized bourbon whiskey and lemon juice as if they were BFFs. "*Merci!* You read my mind."

"*Ce n'était pas mon idée.* It was his request." He gestured to a man standing near the buffet.

A man straight out of the world she thought she'd escaped.

"Oh, no."

"*C'est vrai.*"

Bindi could avoid him—dive into the waiter's shadow,

duck past the couple gyrating perilously close to a curio cabinet stocked with valuable Cora Island knickknacks, shimmy out to the east wing of the veranda and slink her way to the estate's private, lush tropical garden.

Except her ex-fiancé's eldest son shared his single-minded, addictive personality, and if Santino Franco was bent on destroying her party, avoidance wouldn't dissuade him.

Besides that, she had every right to this Seychelles holiday, and *he* was the trespasser.

When she'd become engaged to Alessandro, neither of his sons had welcomed her into the Franco circle. Okay, she could understand their reluctance to accept her as stepmommy number three. And yes, it might've seemed unconventional, since she was several years younger than both Santino and his brother, Nate. But from the get-go their harsh resentment had haunted whatever seedlings of hope she'd harbored of a legit relationship with their father.

Nate had once been an ally, but generally he'd kept his distance. With Santino, there'd never been any give or compromise or chance of more existing between them than utter distrust. Which was a pity, because he was the type of man she would normally admire. Perhaps she did anyway. Just a bit.

For months they'd lived under the same roof, intertwined their lives, and yet his eyes had always held suspicion when they touched her. Every degrading thing he left unspoken surfaced in that grave, uncompromising gaze.

"Shall I give him your thanks?"

Bindi bussed the waiter's cheeks. "No, I'll do it." Plucking the cherry from the glass, rolling it around in her mouth and relishing its sweetness, she considered her next move.

Somewhere in the silence of Santino's humorless face, hidden beneath his well-cut clothes and resting behind his steel-muscled frame was the man's compassion.

Of that she had no doubt.

As she approached, she felt something coast over her like an invisible stroke. She thought she'd felt it before, in the past, but hadn't tried to place it then.

Was it interest?

"Bindi. You were blonde in Las Vegas." His voice was even deeper and rougher than she remembered. That stroking sensation swept over her again.

"My father's a quarter Native American, a quarter Polish and half African-American. My mother was born a half Armenian, half German Jew. I'm not a natural blonde."

Rather than make some insensitive remark, Santino just nodded—and she appreciated that.

Alessandro Franco was an Italian Catholic, and his first wife, Gloria, an African-American Christian. Their sons had experienced a blended heritage.

Bindi hadn't.

On paper, she was the *other* checkbox. The unexplained. It diminished the beauty of her patchwork heritage, but so did plenty of her parents' deliberate choices. Focus on tomorrow, not yesterday, was Roscoe and Daphne's mantra. Assimilation, civil wars and debates about anything from places of worship to racial slurs received no respect when there were political opportunities to secure their present and future comforts.

"Sending me this drink. Is this some sort of passive-aggressive gesture—?"

Santino stripped the drink from her grasp and took a swallow. "Damn, that's some good whiskey."

"I didn't say I didn't want it," she protested, reclaiming the glass to take a sip herself.

*Yum.* There weren't many things she and Santino Franco agreed on, but apparently quality whiskey was one of them.

"How did you know I was here?"

"I remembered," he said after an uncomfortable stretch of silence during which he simply stared at her. "Dad asked you to plan this trip a while ago. You were happy."

"Enamored, really," she said. No part of being a man's doll, of swapping her self-respect for money and gifts, had ever made her happy.

Toe-to-toe now, she raised her chin to rest her gaze against his. Would he raid the estate, send her guests scrambling off the premises like ants brushed off a cube of sugar? "It's Valentine's. Poisoning my guests against me will bring down my V-Day buzz." It was jokingly said, but when she spoke next, there was nothing to buffer her sincerity. "I don't know why you're here, Santino, but these people have nothing to do with you and me. They're having a good time. Please don't ruin this for them."

"I'm not here to ruin your party."

She hadn't expected that, and it took her a moment to regroup. "Why *are* you here?"

People scooted past, wormed around them in search of refreshments. Nudging, jostling, they created chaos— yet Santino didn't budge. Until he leaned close to Bindi. "If we were alone, I'd tell you why. Can I do that? Get you alone?"

*Absolutely not.* "Yes."

"When?"

"Later."

"And that'd give you a head start? Your mind got busy figuring out an escape route the second you realized I was here."

"I—"

"Dare you to lie."

*Damn you, Franco.* "I won't take off," she decided. "Eat. Drink. See this?" Bindi ensnared his key pendant, tangling her fingers in the chain. "Go find a few locks to put this in. That's how the game works. You want a connection? Time with someone tonight? Unlock her first."

"Including you?"

"Including me." He was just taunting her, right? He hated her. Bindi let the key drop, because it suddenly felt hot against her skin. Or had the heat only transferred from his chest to her fingers?

"Bindi."

*Walk away*, she commanded her feet. But they were working against her. In fact, her entire body was. Whiskey in hand, she froze right there in front of the man she didn't want on her island or anywhere in her temporary dreamworld.

Santino said her name again, but she felt it more than heard it. The word was an abrasive vibration in her ear, because he was close…

Too close, yet somehow not close enough.

Tanned, large-knuckled fingers brushed her as they sought her necklace. A tug on the silver lock jerked her out of her stupor, but it brought her forward, into his heat.

Had he always been so…hot? Not just a wicked heat source on a February island night, but darkly sexy?

Dressed as though he'd purposely stopped short of polished, he wore designer clothes, but the shirt's open collar and rolled sleeves offered teasing peeks at crisp chest hair and tattooed, vein-crisscrossed arms. His wavy silver-at-the-temples dark hair was tamed into a short ponytail that she ached to work loose.

The low set of his brow and that crooked nose? She couldn't imagine him without them. Framing his narrow, dangerous mouth was a beard that loitered at the midway point between five-o'clock shadow and deliberate scruff—just enough whiskers to leave behind a rosy sting on her throat, breasts, thighs…

*Don't go there.* Bindi abandoned that train of thought before her mind began drawing erotic pictures of what his strong hands might be capable of. But his key was already nestled tight in her lock.

*Twist.*

*Click.*

And she was his. Sort of. It was only a game, and in her reality, fair gameplay didn't exist.

Disentangling their necklaces, she whispered, "This is the master lock, you could say. *Every* key unlocks this lock."

"Who unlocked you?"

As if she'd divulge that he'd been the only man she allowed close enough to try? "You're here to discuss Al. Your father. My ex-fiancé." That man had burst all of Bindi's illusions and had almost taken Santino's life. He'd brought them together but would always stand between them.

"Bindi, he's gone. Where is he?"

Casting a sharp glance about them, she growled, "I don't know."

Al had disappeared from Nevada over two weeks ago, something she'd found out when investigators had approached her for questioning. Every time someone attached her to his wrongdoings she'd more firmly regretted that she'd let herself fall for his money.

If she could hazard a guess, she'd suggest he was holed up in a safe house on some Mediterranean island, sleeping soundly through heavenly sunrises and toasting the sunsets with wine and fluffy Italian pastries.

"Maybe I don't believe you."

"Feel free to not believe me all the way back to Mahé and back to the US." She turned.

*"Bindi."*

She stopped when he said her name as though it were a plea or a prayer. The word was firm yet gentle, his voice completely broken down.

"I'm sorry."

"Are you?"

"Yeah. My temper and yours were meant for each other."

But she wasn't meant for him, or any man. She was too much trouble, had too many—what was it her mother frequently said?—*issues*. She had too many issues.

Desperate to settle her focus on anything but Santino, Bindi started to cross the room but saw the man she'd been drawn to earlier tonight—before crunk music and Santino Franco had turned her 'round and 'round.

She put down the whiskey, followed his Afro to the veranda. A temperate breeze and dozens of twinkling tea lights embraced her. "Are you leaving?"

Pausing, the man started to smile—

"I unlocked her."

Bindi whipped around. *Santino!*

The stranger gave a lackluster bow and mumbled a polite good-night, then hauled ass off the veranda.

"Why did you interfere?"

"I unlocked you," Santino said slowly. "If we're playing your game, that means you're mine tonight. You owe me time."

"We'll discuss Al *after* the party reaches its natural conclusion."

"When is that?"

"Usually parties fizzle when either the food or liquor is gone," she said, selecting a pillar to drop against.

The tea lights teased the shadows as he entered her space.

Countering, "Would it conclude early if I were to walk back in that house and start telling your new friends why I'm here?" he waited for a reaction.

If he wanted fear, he wouldn't get it. No man would wield that power over her again. "You're not going to do that," she predicted. "You already said you wouldn't."

"How can you trust that I didn't lie?"

"Lying isn't in your repertoire," she said. Lying was an art her parents and their minions had taught her, but recently she'd decided to start telling the truth. Though she reported to tabloid bloggers, she presented perceptions of the truth that were difficult to discredit. She didn't invent scandal where there was none. Often, there was enough legitimate scandalous material in Nevada and California to make fabrication a wasted effort. "I always liked you for that—your honesty."

"There are things I always liked about you, too, Bindi."

"I won't ask you to list them."

"Great, because I'm going to, and I don't want you to think it's because you asked."

A former NFL superstar who'd kept himself closed off the entire time she'd known him was going to say what he liked about her?

"I like that you're still standing after being hurt."

She had a lot of experience in that department. "I'm resilient. Most people are."

"You buy novelty stuff."

"I'm a junk hoarder. According to my mother."

Watching his face transform as he chuckled almost turned her legs into wet noodles. Mr. Big Bad Strong and Silent could smile like *that*?

It dazzled her, like one of those rare cosmic events. A meteor shower or solar eclipse.

"Junk hoarder, eh? We can go with that. When you moved out of the house, you left some of your things behind. Key chains, pen sleeves, old-fashioned toys—that kind of stuff."

"Then you have my wooden tic-tac-toe game?"

"Last time I saw it, the staff were boxing it all up for you. And that was a couple of months ago. There's only Nadia there now. Everybody else cleared out."

"Where do you live?"

"Vegas."

"I didn't keep tabs." She broke away from his gaze, busied herself appreciating the flickering of the candlelight against the villa's pearl-white exterior. "I decided to break away from that environment—the gold-digging and celebrity lifestyle. In measured steps, I'm changing. Change—you can't absorb it all at once. Bit by bit's the best way."

"If you wanted distance from that environment, why are you here, Bindi? My father paid for this vacation."

She almost hadn't come, had debated for hours. But the trip had already been paid for, with the equivalent of two million US dollars deposited in a Seychelles bank under her name. Cora Island was supposed to give her the chance to get to know herself again, figure out how she'd survive on her feet instead of her back. "I came here to be alone, Santino."

He gestured toward the villa's entrance, indicating the obvious contradiction.

"I didn't want to be alone on Valentine's."

"I get it."

"Ask Nadia to help herself to what's in the box, or donate it to charity with my thanks. I won't be making the drive out to Henderson to get it. I can't go back to Alessandro's house." It held memories of what she thought she'd wanted, in a past life. Once upon a scheme, she'd wanted to marry a wealthy older man, because wealthy older men were all she'd experienced in her young life. She would've earned her own fame, starring in a reality TV show based on her life as an NFL team owner's wife, had Al not sold the team and sold her lies.

But even if she had obtained that life, she'd still cry herself to sleep sometimes. Life was lonely when family closed their doors and friends turned their backs.

"Keep 'em coming—the things you like about me.he said lightly, but the seriousness in his eyes had her heart thudding.

"You're not as selfish as you pretend to be." He glanced toward the crowd. "You told me you didn't want this party ruined for *them*."

How strange of him. Gold diggers didn't have a rep for being altruistic, and often the nuances of a person, the struggles and sacrifices and reasons *why* never came to light. Labels trumped everything, and Santino had never cared about anything except the label he'd given her before they'd even met.

"I don't want it ruined for me, either," she clarified, not exactly sure why she couldn't just accept his words or think nothing of them. "There was a lot of effort. The regular villa staff helped me organize and decorate. They're gone tonight, but I'm proud of their hard work and don't want to see it wasted."

"Gone? Why?"

"I gave them the night off for Valentine's. Hopefully they're all having a nice night in Victoria."

"Bindi?"

"Yes?"

"Generous."

So he liked her resilience, her generosity and that she hoarded novelty knickknacks.

He hadn't called her hot or pretty or gorgeous.

He'd cited qualities that had nothing to do with her appearance, and she slammed into joy the way somebody might walk into a door.

Throat tight, she said, "I—I'm sorry, but…I'm not used to this, Santino. What are we supposed to do with all of this? When I was with…him…you and I— We didn't have civil conversations or freely say what we like about each other." He'd been too guarded, and she too focused on rescuing herself using someone else's fortune. "I came here for clarity, but you show up and…"

"And what?"

"And I'm confused. Sorry."

"I know," he said, and the gentle words were so strange from one of the harshest men she'd ever come across. He stepped closer. "But I can't take it back. I'm not going to do that."

"Then there's that," she whispered, so quietly. The confession hurt, yet it felt as rich as liberty. "I don't want you to take it back."

Bindi made the mistake of meeting him head-on. Key necklace to lock necklace. Eye to eye. Body to body as he used his granite-solid form—shoulders, crotch, thighs, hands—to pin her to the pillar.

"Who unlocked you?"

"You, Santino."

"And?"

"You. Just you."

And then they collided mouth to mouth, with the urgency of heat and demand of whiskey flavoring the taste. Grace and precision weren't welcome in this kiss. It wasn't about intellect or the melding of spirits. Just hard, impenitent want.

Bindi wrapped herself around him: a hand around his ponytail, an arm around his neck, legs parting to invite him deeper. Fingertips sank into flesh. Wet tongues invaded.

This was more than a mistake. This was bad in every naughty, delicious, unforgivable way.

# *Chapter 3*

Santino needed salvation. Kissing Bindi as though he was thirsty for her, pressing against her as though she was meant for him, felt so good it couldn't be anything but wrong. The weak, almost voiceless part of him that clung to decent judgment begged for something to wrest control from whatever instinct had triggered him to get up close and sexual with this woman.

Bindi sank deeper into their kiss and he couldn't move—couldn't let go of her hips, couldn't break away from her mouth. God, her mouth. Lusciously warm. Irresistibly willing. Impossibly familiar. He felt as though he'd already been inside her. He was ready to be, and it floored him. He hadn't been so hard in months.

*Damn it.* Why couldn't she be a stranger, or a standard gold digger? Hell, hooked around him as she was now, she wasn't even his father's ex-fiancée.

She was, in some twisted way, paradise. A perfect fit. She licked him just right, yanked his hair so greedily that he wanted to strip her naked and return the favor. She tasted of whiskey and heat, her scent so crisp and clean it was downright erotic.

She sighed, the sound heavy with frustration and confusion, as though she were searching for something and wasn't sure she'd like what she found.

Because she was in this as deeply as he.

And he was abso-freakin'-lutely fascinated.

Bindi retreated from their kiss. But they remained tangled together in each other's arms. "I can't stand you."

*So the old Bindi, the one who attacks when she feels cornered, resurfaces.*

He was thrown off-kilter with the new Bindi and didn't know how to handle her. He didn't know if he *could* handle her. "Good."

"Good?"

"Yeah. Good that you could take your tongue out of my mouth long enough to say it. Now we can both think." His senses were slowly coming home to him. This kiss, this closeness, was a bad idea. "You hate me. Say it."

Another half frustrated, half confused moan fled her sweet, swollen lips. The tea lights' flames winked around them, but the regret in her pale blue eyes was too bright to mistake. "Why?"

He pressed against her, harder. She gasped. "You're not giving me enough of a reason to let you go."

"What about dislike?"

"*Dislike* is damn near a compliment. Why can't you say the word that'll end this?"

"Loathe," she said, as if he hadn't confronted her with a simple question. "Or detest. Yeah, detest. Go with that."

"*Hate.* Why won't you say it, Bindi?"

"I never hated you."

A first-class lie. But lies came delicately easy to this woman, and after reading her history, it wasn't hard to figure out why she had to take measured steps to get used to telling the truth. "Your body's against me, and your taste's in my mouth, but let's remember the facts." He said it for his own sake as much as hers. "Marriage?

A straight shot to Dad's money? A reality TV show? C'mon…did you think I'd let that happen?"

"Al ended things."

"Saving me the effort." Even if his father hadn't strung Bindi along—keeping her in the Franco mansion while he wagered what he didn't spend on high-caliber call girls— only to ultimately drop her, Santino would've crushed their wedding bells.

Bindi had chased a prenup-free marriage, had plotted to become an instant celebrity as she exploited the Las Vegas Slayers with a reality TV program.

And while Santino was busy protecting his father from yet another fame-hungry fiancée, Al was making dirty deals, selling the team and ushering them both into separate chambers of hell.

"I got in your way. I blocked. I pushed. I wasn't going to let up until you were out of Dad's life. You hated me for that."

"It's safe to drop that mission now, Santino. I *am* out of Al's life. He hasn't phoned or emailed or sent a message by pigeon." Bindi uncurled her fingers from his hair, and he stupidly began to miss the needy force of her tugging. "And okay, I'm not going to deny it—I *did* hate you."

"You don't now? What changed?"

"The truth, as I saw it. And I changed. I'm not going to let myself feel *anything* for a Franco—even hate."

Another lie threaded into her words. She might not hate—or loathe or detest—him, but the tremble of her thighs whispered all kinds of secret feelings.

Seeking what she wouldn't admit, he slowly brought one hand forward, curving his fingers when they met the softness of her ass.

*Stop me, Bindi, because I can't stop myself.*

But she didn't.

A bit of determined maneuvering, and he had his index finger raking up and down the crotch of her thong.

"Franco, you're playing with me."

Pressing against her, he said, "Playing's fun, Paxton. When you're winning, I mean."

"Who says you're winning?"

"You."

She began to shake her head, but another deliberate brush of his finger had her blurting, "Okay. Damn it, okay. Just—"

"What? Just what?"

"Hating you would be less complicated than this." Her face was so serious—her eyes so troubled. "Just touch me. Would you do that, Santino? I want to know what it's like."

"You've been touched before."

"I've never asked. I've never had to ask."

"Don't say you feel nothing, because I know it's a lie," he said, moving aside damp fabric to stroke into her. "You're wet. I wouldn't call that *feeling nothing*."

Bindi swallowed, and he didn't doubt she was silencing a pleasured sound he'd earned the right to hear. "Stop—please. I'm afraid."

"Of me?" But he backed off instantly.

"Yes. And of me, and emotions and real feelings. I can't spare them, because if I do and you hurt me... Don't ask me to, okay?" She pushed away from the pillar behind her and he stepped away to give her more room. "I'm going to the garden."

"We need to talk."

"About Al," she allowed. "Not about that kiss. Not about the trouble *this*—" she thumped her silver lock necklace "—caused tonight."

"And your party?"

Righting her dress, she scoffed. "We're all adults, capable of being left to our own devices." She waved a hand skyward. "A storm's coming. Nothing to freak about, but if I was a gambler I'd place a bet on my guests clearing out before the rain starts."

"Think I'm going to follow their lead?"

"It'd be smart if you did."

"And forfeit my reward for unlocking you?"

"Isn't a kiss enough?" She started to strut to the east end of the veranda. "Come on—really. We weren't going to take this past flirting."

She didn't know how damn wrong she was. And she'd saved them both by stopping their kiss when she had.

Bindi went from strut to speed walking, and he didn't get in her way this time. Now that he knew her dark hair and tempting shape, knew her delicate scent, knew that she was off guard, catching her again would be easy.

He'd kind of liked playing with her.

As the door swung open, noise flooded the veranda and people trickled outside. A man frowning at his smartphone paced back and forth before a woman summoned him to where she rested against a pillar.

*That damn pillar.*

Seeing Bindi Paxton wedged up against the wide column with her blue eyes fixed on him, Santino cursed cruelly and started walking.

He didn't seek her right away. First he had to remember that he was a near-forty man whose life had been Express Mailed to an inferno and for Bindi, sex was a bargaining chip. Second, he had to remember that there was a chance that Bindi had been a part of what his father had done. Only time would tell if she was innocent of that sordid mess.

As far as he, his brother and the mansion's cast of household staff knew, Bindi had made herself "access denied" to Alessandro. She'd accept his ring, live in his house and dress herself in the revealing clothes the man preferred she wear, but there'd be no sex before the wedding night.

With each other or anyone else.

If Santino had her pegged right, she liked sex and hadn't taken a hiatus from it for religious beliefs or the glory of a chaste engagement. Point blank, saying no was her right and whoever didn't agree had the right to go screw themselves.

Santino had ignored the staff's crude jokes that gushed with vulgarities such as *blue balls* and *worn out right hand* and suggestions that Al cheat on Bindi rather than marry her for a five-minute consummation. Even through the red haze of his own pain, he could recognize their engagement as a business transaction that'd end as Al's second and third marriages had—in expensive, intrusive courtroom proceedings.

And sometimes he had his doubts about Al and Bindi's sexless engagement. Something didn't ring true about Al satisfying Bindi's extravagant tastes without compensation.

Santino didn't want to care—regretted that he did. He wished his interlude with Bindi had felt depraved, perverse. Instead it had felt right.

Striding through the night, he heard sand-sprinkled grass crinkle under his shoes and he could sense the threat of rain. Villa Soleil's garden was a stamp of land crowded with tropical trees, plants, bushes and bursts of flowers he couldn't begin to identify.

Bindi, who'd built a topiary hobby from her admiration for horticulture and freakish flair for cutting things, seemed at fragile peace in this garden.

Her skin glimmered golden in the gentle landscape lamps that lit his path to the fountain where she sat on the edge, her fingers dancing through a slender stream of water. "Ever visited the Bellagio's botanical gardens?"

"Probably." He'd lived in Las Vegas his entire life, maintaining an off-season condo that he'd shared with his girlfriend. The Bellagio was a popular spot for business meals, and Tabitha had dragged him there often enough for various celebrations.

Tabitha. Maybe she was the reason he couldn't—wouldn't—remember clearly.

"Well, if you can't picture the Bellagio's gardens, my comparison will mean zero."

"Compare anyway. I might surprise you."

"Surprise me *again*, you mean. Crashing my party, kissing me on the veranda—surprises." She cleared her throat. "The Bellagio's conservatory and the gardens are magnificent. At Christmastime it's all surreal. This garden's not perfect—it's not arranged very strategically, which is a shame, because these orchids should be showcased—but Cora Island's not manicured. It's more of a jungle. Rugged. Sort of how I imagine the Garden of Eden." She shook droplets of water from her fingertips, shrugged. "Even this gorgeous garden, which was obviously designed more for privacy than out of consideration for these poor incense trees' prosperity, is—"

"Wild."

A gasp of laughter rang throughout the garden. Nodding, she said, "Wild, exactly."

"We shared the same thought?"

"Weirder things have happened. It can be our secret.

What we did earlier, getting carried away with locks and keys, can be a secret, too."

Keeping secrets with this woman sounded like trouble, but he craved it anyway.

"You didn't ask if I'm with somebody."

"Because I already know you'd never damage a relationship that way."

Tabitha had killed the version of Santino who'd bought into the *relationship* hype—and he should thank her for that. Not that he'd ever be okay with his girlfriend sabotaging their future together the minute she realized surgery and rehab wouldn't be enough to get him back onto the field. But in the time since he'd read her "I can't do this anymore, sorry" text message in the recovery room, smashed his phone and been restrained and doped up with sedatives to control his dangerous behavior, he'd gotten used to complacency.

Kissing Bindi had shocked his system.

"Are you free?" he asked.

"Indefinitely. Being single suits me."

"The dude with the piercings. Who's he?"

"A stranger. I wanted time with him." She watched him intently now. "Maybe I'll get it, after the storm comes and goes and after you leave this island."

Santino didn't intend to leave Cora Island without Bindi. Except telling her that would put them at odds—and him behind the damn eight ball. "Your guests are starting to clear out. Wanna get back in there?"

Bindi frowned at him. "What, that's it? I say I might spend time with someone else, and you have no reaction?"

"What reaction do you want?"

"Not this coldness. You kissed me."

"And you said you're afraid."

"I am. I'm afraid of what tomorrow will look like if we take things too far." She quit toying with the water, and her damp fingers were on his wrist, urging him nearer. "But passing up what could happen tonight? That terrifies me."

Bindi's fingers moved to his abdomen, lower to drag down his zipper. Part of him considered backing away, but the majority of him wanted her to know why he couldn't give her what she wanted from a man.

After a few moments of stroking him, she put her hands in her lap. "What's going on?"

Swearing, Santino zipped his pants, then yanked the band from his hair just to rake it into a short ponytail again. "It's not clear to you?"

"That you don't want me? I'm starting to realize that."

"Bindi, you know my father offered a bounty that killed my career."

Her eyes narrowed. "But you seem to be in great shape now, so…?"

Lucky SOB, his former teammates called him. To them, erectile dysfunction was the lesser of the evils when stacked against what he could've endured. Past a year postinjury, he was strong—as healed as he'd ever be—but he wasn't whole. "Spinal damage," he said. "Pulverized disc. Nicked cord."

"Does your back hurt?" she pressed. Those narrowed eyes suddenly popped open wide, searched his frantically. "Wait. Can you get an erection?"

"I can't sustain it or get one at all without focus. So the mistakes you might want to make tonight—they can't be made with me."

Bindi brought her fingers back to the water. "So you *did* come here to interrogate me about Al."

"I need your help. I need you to come back to Las Vegas with me to find him."

"I can't go back to that world again. Half of me wants to leave Vegas altogether, start over fresh somewhere else… Somewhere like this island, where there are wild gardens."

"There are trees and orchids in Las Vegas."

"Not at my fingertips. Not anymore. I live downtown, on East Dune. My apartment building's grounds are managed by an insecticide-happy company, and a girl can expect only so much from windowsill plants and Chia Pets."

In less than a year she'd gone from sculpting topiaries in front of a Forbes-featured mega mansion to fussing over Chia Pets in a downtown Vegas apartment.

Fact was, instability shouldn't be new to her. According to the report he'd taken from Zaf, her parents had pulled her out of a private elementary school following a tightly classified drug overdose incident. The barebones story was simple: prominent politician's daughter gets into a medicine cabinet, overdoses at school, the school and local hospital receive prestigious awards and private donations and the daughter gets quietly homeschooled until college. Then she'd popped up on the radar again when she had been kicked off her Illinois congressman father's campaign team after getting herself expelled from college and leaking proof of the United States' "Boy Scout Politician" Senator Paxton's affair with a staff member. She'd spent the years since scouting the country for elderly men wealthy enough to afford her attention.

A hell of a ride, but she was at the end of the road if she'd dyed her hair and traveled to Cora Island to meet up with his father.

He might be off base, and if he was he'd apologize. But he had a damn solid reason to be suspicious. She'd sold out before. Who was to say her loyalty couldn't be bought again?

"Who's watering the windowsill plants and Chia Pets while you're hanging out on the Seychelles?" he asked.

"My budget's got no room for hired help, so no plant-sitter. If leaving them to fend for themselves turns out to be as selfish as you seem to want me to believe, I'd like to think they'd be forgiving. Two weeks isn't forever."

Two weeks, meaning she was expecting to stay on the Seychelles another seven days.

He needed her on a US-bound flight tomorrow afternoon. If Al intended to persuade or pressure her face-to-face to aid in his escape, he'd need to bring his ass back to Las Vegas to get to her.

"Bindi, I can't let you stay here another week."

"Didn't we already establish that I'm free? *Free*, as in no one has a hold on me. No one has the authority to say what he will or won't 'let' me do."

"Look at it this way. The FBI, NFL and gaming commission come down on my father and he disappears. No trace of him—just gone. Couple of weeks later, you, his ex-fiancée, dye your hair and skip the country for an island trip he paid for."

"This vacation was arranged before Al was charged."

"Is that supposed to make a difference to the media? These people hunt blood. They won't relent until your every secret's cracked open and manipulated so well that even you can't distinguish the truth from the lies. Hell, this ain't a reality TV show. It's cold reality and it's a bastard." Santino touched her lace-covered shoulder when she started to get up. "Prove you're not running or hiding. Help me find him."

"How? Not saying I will…but how?"

"Come back to Las Vegas with me. If he's after you, let him find you there."

"Wow. Drop everything, go back to Vegas with you and make myself bait. And when would I do all this?"

"Tomorrow."

She jerked free of him. "I'm more concerned with tonight. There's a party waiting for me. I'm not going to sacrifice it for a guy who I heard can't exactly finish what he starts."

She could've put all her strength behind a slap to his face and it wouldn't have lodged into him as painfully as her words. But when Bindi lashed out, it usually backfired. Using his weakness as a weapon only shined a light on her desperation.

"I can't leave this house without an answer, Bindi. Give me that, then we'll see about finishing what *we* started."

"Leave the chocolate fountain."

At the words *chocolate fountain*, Bindi, who'd returned from the garden to invest her energies into mingling, avoiding Santino Franco and then sending off the stragglers determined to use Villa Soleil as shelter from the rainstorm, stopped dead at the edge of the ornately carved arch in the dividing wall between the living and dining rooms.

Wiggling her ears as if to sharpen their eavesdropping ability, she ducked and peered in. The disheveled furniture and improperly discarded trash were marks of a party hosted well. She'd compensated the serving/ cleaning staff in advance to discreetly sweep for condoms and other paraphernalia that suggested guests had taken tonight's lock-and-key icebreaker and aphrodisiac-themed menu to extreme levels.

As she herself had done with Santino on the veranda, where anyone could've seen them. A helluva souvenir that pillar would make—except she was committed to scrubbing her memory clean of his finger teasing her wet core, testing her judgment.

Damn, the man could make her hot.

But they were going to have serious words if he was thinking about going open season on the fountain. She'd pined for the white and dark chocolate streams, but with the house so crowded she hadn't found a chance to make a pig out of herself.

Faking cheer, she entered the living room and smiled at the headwaiter. "What about the fountain?"

*"Le monsieur—"*

"I asked him to leave it," Santino smoothly interrupted. Addressing the waiter, he said, "The hostess has it bad for middle-of-the-night sweets."

She felt her skin tingle, could almost see a deep pink flush spreading across her cheeks. She had a weakness for chocolate sin, but didn't usually let herself give in until late at night. Or early in the morning—however anyone wanted to look at it. What did *he* know about it, though?

"You didn't bring any marshmallows and graham crackers, did you?" Santino said to the waiter, but he was watching her.

Chocolate, marshmallows, graham crackers. S'mores.

Godiva chocolate s'mores.

*"Non, monsieur."*

"No problem. Just leave the fountain," Bindi said kindly. When he moved on to another task, she eyed Santino.

"Pissed off, huh?" A casual shrug of his solid, broad shoulders. "I didn't tell him you go buck wild on s'mores."

"Why reference them at all?"

"I remembered you like them."

"Then, why did you remember?" Why did he remember catching her in a vulnerable moment? Why did he remember that, struck off guard with embarrassment and a brush of something she'd never analyzed, she'd been friendly to him? "God, Santino, *stop.* Whatever game or strategy this is—stop."

He turned, and then he was facing her and her blood was surging hot and she didn't doubt he knew she was horny.

What if this had nothing to do with the man and everything to do with her? She'd restricted herself with a sex-free engagement. After that ended, she'd become so disgusted with the men from her past who'd damaged her that she'd temporarily lost the appetite for it.

Arousal must've been stirring for months, and now it had reached boiling point.

"It's after midnight and I'm waiting for an answer. Are you going back to Vegas with me?"

Alessandro Franco was once her connection to Las Vegas elite, her ticket to a reality television show. Now his drama threatened to give her hives. She'd almost legally tied herself to a man who'd paid someone to nearly paralyze his son.

"WTF" didn't even scratch the surface of the questions she asked herself. And here was Santino, demanding answers.

A groan of thunder startled her.

"All right?" he asked.

"Of course."

"I…" Visibly alarmed by his own give-a-damn, he

nodded. As if it'd do either of them any favors for him to start thinking he might give a damn about her.

Alessandro and his sons weren't the most considerate of men. The three of them were dominant, cocky males. See. Want. Take. Move along. That was how they operated, and it wasn't likely to change for her.

Al and Nate had each extracted her trust, abused it and left her to recover from the scuffs.

Santino would, too. Once he got her embedded in his search for Al, he'd use her, then cut her down.

"The answer's no. I won't help you."

"Hasty decisions can cost a person."

"Oh, yeah? What's it going to cost me?"

"Your reputation, for one."

"Yes, my saintly reputation." She giggled at the ludicrousness of it. "What else?"

"Protection. If Dad gets you roped into his shit, who's going to save you?"

She simply wouldn't get roped in, no matter what promises and money Alessandro offered, but if she hadn't convinced Santino of that before, she had slim chances of succeeding now.

"Legal defense doesn't come cheap. There's the truth, and that does matter. But what the right people *think* is the truth matters more. Let doubt against you get lodged in deep in folks' minds, and you'll have one hell of an expensive battle in front of you."

"I learned that lesson already. My father's a politician."

"Good ol' Senator Roscoe Paxton. Where was he when you were being questioned about Dad and Gian DiGorgio? Where was he for all your other indiscretions?"

"In Illinois, confident that he raised a self-reliant

daughter. I didn't boo hoo to Daddy and Mommy. As I said before, I can save myself."

The lie had come automatically. Bindi wasn't about to confess that her parents' anger toward her had reached new heights when she'd called them last summer after news broke about her ex's illegal deeds. Grudgingly her mother had wired her funds to hire a lawyer.

"We can't be connected to that man's crimes. Your father gave away his Bears season tickets because so many reporters have bombarded him for comments about your connection to the Las Vegas Slayers." Daphne had sounded regretful, as always. Was there anything in her life she didn't regret? "Bindi, I hate this."

"Me, too. As soon as I can, I'll take a flight to Midway."

"Why?"

"To come home. So you, Daddy and I can start fresh."

Daphne had sighed. "Oh. Oh, Bindi, no. I meant I hate that I'm your mother. It's only because we're not the best parent-child match… Oh, you're quiet. You're offended? Oh, don't get yourself offended. It's just that you have… issues. Even as a girl you were complicated. And Roscoe and I probably weren't the best candidates to raise a child with so many *issues*. My therapist explained it much more articulately."

Add in another sigh or two, a few more gutting insults and a flat-out order to never reach out to Roscoe or Daphne again, and that summed up Bindi's last conversation with her parents.

Crossing his arms, Santino said, "Beep. Beep. Beep."

"What the hell?"

"I've got a bullshit detector and right now it's going crazy."

"Ha. If you had one, it should've self-destructed when

Al told you the Blues forced him to sell the Slayers. But you believed those lies, just as I did, and now he's hit the road and you're begging me for a favor."

"And if your family had your back, you wouldn't be growing Chia Pets in a stripper's apartment."

Bindi's eyes narrowed, and she sensed something she didn't like. "How'd you know about my apartment?"

"You said you live on East Dune. That street's infested with exotic dancers and porn stars, so that was a guess. A good one."

And did he judge her for that? She searched for condescension, but saw a stress-beaten man. A *sexy* stress-beaten man.

"About Al. The answer's no. Okay?" Before he could get another persuasive word in edgewise, she said, "There aren't any boat transfers to Mahé this late, and you're grounded in this storm. A clever guy like you must've reserved a room at the hotel…right?"

"No."

Oh, crap.

"Then an attractive guy like you must've unlocked someone who'd let you get in her bed tonight."

"Seemed an asshole thing to do, getting in another woman's bed knowing I'd be thinking about you."

"Me?"

"Mmm-hmm."

Outside the wind entwined with the rain, and the tea lights flickering on the veranda were barely a memory. Indoors were the faint sounds of water running in another room, voices issuing orders back and forth and the footsteps of servers finishing their tasks for the night.

He stepped forward. Directly behind her was a chocolate fountain, so she couldn't step backward. "Tonight I learned your taste, how soft the skin on your thighs is, what it feels like to open you with my finger. I'm not going to blank slate that by getting in another woman's bed."

*Oy.* Silk wasn't made to withstand this kind of blunt talk, so her panties were either becoming soaked straight through or were simply dissolving.

"It's wrong."

"Gotta be," he agreed as his mouth found her earlobe and the hard front of him pressed against her. Hard… He was *hard*. Just like before. It made her wonder if it actually *wouldn't* be a problem. "Why does it feel so good to do the wrong thing?"

"Not always." If he'd ever done wrong—horribly, reprehensibly wrong, as she had—he'd know the greasy, treacherous feeling she battled every day.

Years ago, she'd offered herself, then her father, as media chow. She'd had her desperate reasons then, just as she'd had when she leaked T and A photos of the Las Vegas Slayers' female athletic trainer. Now she freelanced as a celebrity news rat for food and shelter—and gently used designer clothes on eBay. She sniffed for juicy scandals, he said/she said gossip and dirty pics and vids, then sold her findings to a team of TMZ-wannabe bloggers.

Resisting his closeness, because the man had enough troubles without getting mixed up with someone like her, she said, "We can't be standing close like this. There are people here, and I don't perform for audiences. And the answer's still no. Alessandro saw me as just a gold-digging sex object, not an accomplice or a confidant."

"He was going to marry—"

"He wasn't. There was no love in that relationship. None. At most, there was pity and respect and trust—

*cautious* trust, and even that was one-sided. So it'd be pointless to think I could lure him out of hiding." She almost pressed her palms to his chest, but didn't want to risk unconsciously unbuttoning his shirt. "He's got people in Bologna. Go to Italy, appeal to them."

"I'm appealing to you."

*Yes, you are.*

"Reconsider, Bindi."

She wouldn't. "Rain hasn't shut down short-distance travel, so you're welcome to see if Cora Island's hotel staff might make a check-in exception for you."

"Am I welcome to stay?"

"What?"

"Stay. In case one of your guests decides to pay you an unwanted visit tonight."

"Hilarious." If *hilarious* was synonymous with *dangerous.* The attraction between them was vicious, and the more they baited it, the hungrier it became. "There's a security system."

"Don't be naive."

"I'm not. I'm pointing out what a crappy excuse that is. You never lied to me before. Don't start now."

A frown flickered at his mouth.

"What you mean is in case *Alessandro* decides to pay a visit." At his silence, she growled, "For the gazillionth time, this isn't some Bonnie and Clyde story. I'm not involved. But go ahead. Stay here tonight—on the sofa—and find out for yourself." She edged around him and stalked back into the house. All she wanted to do was send the staff off and go to bed—alone. Once he left Villa Soleil, she could start taking her life in measured, emotionless steps.

After the last of the servers finally left, she returned to the now-neatened living room. Someone had even restocked the fruit, pretzels and marshmallows that waited under glass domes.

"Can a guest call dibs on the pretzels?"

"You were never a guest, and I'm not playing hostess anymore," she said to Santino as he reentered the room. "I activated the alarm system. Terrace access only. I'm going to bed. But is there something you need?"

"Got caffeine?"

"Lots. There's TV. And this." She indicated the piano that sat in a corner. It didn't resemble the sleek, seductive black baby grand he'd played at the Franco mansion, but it had a quiet regal quality about it. On her first day on the island, she'd returned from a diving excursion, found herself lonely and had kneeled on the oversize bench to tap out a tune. "Play. It deserves a worthy musician to make up for the mess I made of a Yiddish lullaby."

"A Yiddish lullaby?"

"It was more sophisticated than 'Twinkle, Twinkle, Little Star,' which I'm kick-ass good at." For a moment she heard her grandmother's voice hum the comforting melody, and something inside her began to hurt. "There're blankets in the trunk next to the sofa and a three-piece bath before the mudroom."

"Thank you."

"You're thanking me? But I denied you what you wanted."

"It's your right to say no."

Not many of the men she'd had run-ins with would agree with that.

"I'm hoping that when you lock yourself upstairs and get in your bed, you'll think about the bigger picture and you'll change you mind."

"And if I don't? What will you do about it?"

"I won't force you, Bindi. With me, you'll always get options."

Yes, she had options. Right now she had the option to stay with him in this room or go upstairs alone. Risk or safety.

Choosing safety, Bindi went upstairs.

# Chapter 4

She should've taken the chocolate. And the fruit. And the pretzels.

Perhaps if she had, she wouldn't be pacing her darkened suite barefoot scarcely an hour after putting a flight of stairs and a locked door between Santino and herself. Piano music and the sound of rain striking glass battled for dominance. The piece seemed too aggressive, exposing and gut-wrenching to be called *beautiful*. The word was overused anyway, and everyone had a different perception of its meaning.

The music didn't bother her.

Restlessness did.

The Valentine's Day romance seeping from the luxurious decor was getting on her nerves. The suite's elegant wine-and-chocolate offerings had met their demise the previous night while she'd binge-watched an English-subtitled French sitcom, so she was in crisis.

No sweets.

One hand clasped the lock pendant resting between her breasts as the other disengaged the lock on the door.

The song's violently fast tempo, the keys' response to punishing strike of Santino's fingers, provoked her to descend the stairs eagerly. Anticipation escorted her through the shadows to the only room that carried any light.

A golden blush draped the piano and extended only as far as the center of the room, leaving the chocolate fountain in semidarkness.

So tidy, the room appeared as though it hadn't witnessed the havoc of her Valentine's Day party. But the sofa was disheveled. Throw pillows were disarranged. A blanket trailed from the cushions to the floor.

As she selected a cherry and poked it into the white-chocolate waterfall, she observed him. His fixation on the piano dared her to interfere. Worm her way over and cover his hands, maybe. Or dab some chocolate on his bristly jaw and lick it off. Better yet, undo his wavy hair and tug on it. Would it break his concentration if she did that?

"Hey, Franco," she said to his back, loudly enough to overtake the music. "Sofa not comfy enough for you?"

"It's good."

Yet he wasn't relaxed. Tension was in the set of his shoulders and the tightness in his clipped response.

Was he nocturnal or insomniac?

Sympathy flared. As a kid she'd been burdened with anxiety-related sleep problems—nightmares and bed-wetting—triggered by unfamiliar environments. When she hadn't outgrown it by age seven, her father had sent her to sleepaway summer camp with special "grown-up vitamins," which she'd eventually realized had been her mother's Valium. As she conquered the sleep difficulties, she'd met a new landscape of problems that had culminated in an accidental OD. She'd been so stubborn about delivering the lies that had been scripted for her to recite to hospital staff and guidance counselors, such a disappointingly unreliable liar, that she'd left her frustrated parents no other choice than to homeschool her. It'd taken them two years to wean her off the "vitamins" and transfer her dependency to something more socially acceptable.

She sucked the fruit clean, dropped it onto a napkin and drizzled another cherry with dark chocolate.

"The way you stomped up those stairs and slammed the door," he said, not hassling himself to disrupt his playing, "I didn't think you'd be coming back down."

An especially fat cherry stood out among the rest. Grabbing the stem, she smothered it in a profane amount of chocolate and carried it across the room. She joined him on the bench, but with her back facing the piano. "I love chocolate more than I despise you."

The fringes of her vision captured the slow turn of his head, toward her, then back to the piano's keys. At least she'd made a dent in his focus.

"*Detest* was the word you picked."

"Does it matter?" she asked, ripping off the cherry's stem and polishing off the dessert. "It's all the same."

"Except *hate*, right?"

Attraction aside, she'd respected his honesty. Kind of envied it, too. It took massive balls to be honest. Of the Franco men, he was the most direct. Dependable. She couldn't hate him for that.

As he hammered out soul-startling notes, she imagined finding bruises on the keys. The piano's howls drowned the sounds of rain and her own rushing heartbeat.

"I've heard that musicians sometimes use their music to speak for them," she said, raising her voice high. "This piece says you're pissed off."

"Wouldn't you be, if you were me?"

"If you're fishing for perk-me-up compliments, this pond's all dried up," she said. "You're you, but *I'm me*. Age thirty, washed up, undeserving of Chia Pets. At rock bottom I reach out to my family and find out they want nothing to do with me. My friends are actually frenemies. I've got no prospects. And I'm on a glorious vacation because my fugitive ex neglected to have the reservations canceled."

"So you lied earlier. About being tight with your family."

"It's hard to stare a truth that sad in the face twenty-four hours a day, seven days a week. Maybe I should turn around on this bench and play a pissed-off anthem with you."

"Or give that lullaby of yours another try?" When she didn't comment, he asked, "What'd you mean earlier, when you said your mother was born a half Armenian, half German Jew?"

"She converted to Christianity. My grandmother used to say she's still Jewish and that having been born her daughter, I'm Jewish, too, but…I don't really know what I am or where I belong, really."

The lullaby, her grandmother, their connection—all of it was off-limits. Ignoring his suggestion that she give the piano a try, she asked, "Where you live now… Was your baby grand moved there?"

"It's in my father's house."

The Lake Las Vegas mansion was the Franco family home, and where Al's first wife had died. From what Al had shared during one of his sobbing grief episodes that Bindi had promised to keep secret, she gathered that Santino was the heir who'd stood to inherit his father's real estate properties in Las Vegas, Hawaii, Milan and Auckland—in addition to the majority of his assets. Not that his brother would've wanted for anything—co-ownership of a football team and shares of the eyewear manufacturer that had served as Al's original source of wealth weren't anything Bindi would've cried about.

Of course, Al's risky bets, multimillion-dollar losses and desperate deception had distorted whatever they hadn't destroyed.

"What for?" she asked. "It takes a half hour to call a loading company and have a piano carted someplace. Take it back."

"It's just an instrument. Not a necessity."

She couldn't believe that. "It's got a language. It's your voice."

"Tonight's the first time I've played in months."

"Are you going to add this to the list of things you've lost?" Instantly she regretted her words. She truly was—much to Daphne Paxton's chagrin, she was sure—her mother's daughter. "Sorry."

"List, huh? What's on it? NFL career, dignified retirement, inheritance, operations gig in the Slayers' franchise, Dad, Tabitha."

"Al was responsible for all of that *but* Tabitha. She walked. Maybe you never had her to begin with."

"I loved her."

"Transpose the first and last words and you might see that relationship from a different perspective. One that doesn't hurt so much." Twisting around, kneeling behind him on the bench, she had clear intentions. Rest a hand on his shoulder; watch him command the piano. But her fingers ended up freeing his hair and lightly stroking the gray strands at his temples. "Just sex, without love to fog up everything."

"Sex is on the list. You know that."

Of course she did. The spinal cord injury had left behind erectile dysfunction. Just hours ago she'd mentioned it in a Hail Mary attempt to sting his ego and dial back her attraction to him in one shot. "Are you taking meds for ED?"

"No, and never will."

"But… Okay, earlier—when you were holding me—I felt—"

"What?"

*I'm not playing this game. I can't.* "C'mon, Santino…"

"The words. Say the plain words. Don't dress 'em up. What'd you feel?"

"You were hard. I knew, even before you, what you wanted out of that kiss. The mind says one thing. The body contradicts. Can't get them to agree, can you? How do you feel to be torn in two like that, to fight yourself?"

"The same way you feel. We want the same thing right now, don't we?"

She got off the bench and sat on the keys, the noise unexpectedly jarring. "We can't kiss again."

Bindi waited as the music disappeared into the hot silence, her breath held, her thoughts on pause, watching him. His tattooed forearms tensed as he stilled his strong fingers on the piano keys and sent her a slow, challenging smile.

She absorbed that sexy smile and refused to rise to the bait, no matter how tempting it was. "Going there again would be a mistake you don't want to make, Santino."

"Is it a mistake *you* want to make? Is that how you want to play this?"

Caught off guard, she stammered, "This? There is no *this.* Don't start thinking there is. What I mean is, you shouldn't figure a kiss is going to make me more inclined to help you find Al. In fact, I'm less inclined. I'm done with him, and I want to be done with you."

Slowly, each motion tightly controlled, Santino rose

from the bench, crowding her. "Can you last an entire conversation without lying?"

"Yes." *Possibly.*

"Walk away." Bunching the bottom of her dress in his fists, he repeated the grating plea. Again. Once more. "End it."

The soft vibration of his shaking hands stroked through her. "End it? 'Cause your conscience said so?"

"A few months ago, you wore *his* ring."

"A few hours ago, *your* finger was inside me. I let *you* get close. I was wet for *you.*"

"A diamond deposit. He gave you a diamond deposit. A marriage license was your price. If he'd paid your cost, right now you would belong to him."

*Deposit. Price.*

It would've been easier to handle harshness in his voice, not genuine concern. That seared her with shame. She'd been reduced to a commodity, had all but assigned herself a SKU number and dollar amount.

Chest surging, breath light, she slammed her hands down beside her on the keyboard. "I belong to me. That's *always* fact. That wouldn't have changed, even if I'd married him, taken his name and slept with him."

"Bindi." He spread his large hands on her thighs. "Tonight, that's going to be different. 'Cause I need you to belong to me. Get him—get *all* those bastards—out of your head. Or walk away."

This wasn't a transaction, a deal, a trade. What would she gain or lose to give herself freely for once?

"I won't do that, Santino."

Pain crackled in his dark eyes. "Okay."

"I won't walk away."

Heat lunged from their bodies. It was electric, magnetizing. Searching her eyes, he let his hands disappear beneath her dress, snare the straps of her thong and drag it downward. Over her hips. To her knees, where it dropped to her ankles.

"Get Tabitha out of your head." It was her only demand. "Mute her. Ignore her. Because I can take what she can't. *I'm* going to be kneeling in front of you—not her. It's going to be *my* mouth on your body—not hers."

"Sounds fair."

She stepped out of the thong as he stood and shoved the bench back farther. Swearing, he leaned forward and kissed her. So many possibilities were in this teasing, seeking kiss.

But no lies.

Fear whispered that tonight wouldn't be what she needed it to be, but merely a replay of one-night stands past. She'd offer a stellar portrayal of an eager lover, would do what was asked of her, then cry afterward, then her regrets would be eased with pretty gifts and hollow promises.

Or he'd hit it, quit it and be done with it.

Her newfound desire to do what she wanted on her own terms drowned out that whispering fear, demanded she take what she wanted. Right here, right now, with no expectations of any sort of future.

Bindi scooted off the piano. "Sit down. On the bench." She gave his chest a shove, and then it was on to the procedure she'd perfected. Unfasten the belt, open the closure, lower the zip.

"Whoa—oh, God—whoa, whoa," he said as his penis sprang into her hand and she started to work his rigid flesh. "Slow it down."

"Your hard-ons are sometimes-y, so…" She pressed a kiss, added a lick, got a little flushed at the stretch of his shaft and tightening of his sac. "Slowing it down's a luxury we don't have."

What few erections he had must be precious. ED could rob a man of not just "normal" sexual performance, but also a sense of virility and confidence.

A couple of short years ago, Santino had been virility and confidence personified. An NFL star in his prime. A man whose charm and sex appeal she didn't doubt seduced women to touch themselves.

Those women had never had him in the palms of their hands or at the tips of their tongues.

She did—and damned if she wasn't self-satisfied about it.

"Do something for me," he said. "Take off the necklace. Locks and keys don't have anything to do with this."

Together, they lifted the chains over their heads and tossed the necklaces. As she unpinned her hair and shook it out to sweep across her shoulders, he stripped off his shirt.

*Amazing body.*

"Do something for me now," she said, taking off his shoes and socks and tugging at his pants because she was so anxious to get him completely naked. "Tell me what you like. Communication's *so* sexy."

Groaning, he clasped her head, rocking gently against her mouth as she took him deep. "Bindi...I haven't been this hard in... Baby, look, if I can't keep this going, if I can't get off, then so be it."

She rested her forearms on his thighs, kissed his pecs. "How's your back?"

"Stronger. Getting all considerate on me, Paxton?"

"On the veranda, you had me off my feet for a while. I'm no feather."

Her slender, somewhat sylphlike form deceived most.

She had height, curves and an outdoorsy athleticism that contributed muscles to her solid sort of heaviness.

"Definitely not a feather," he agreed. "Durable."

"Very."

"Come here, then. Get closer." Guiding her up, he gripped her hips as she straddled him with her knees on the bench. A sudden slap on her fanny drew a surprised yelp.

He'd slapped her ass.

"Still durable?" he checked.

"Incredibly," she said. "If I rifle through your pockets, will I find any condoms?"

"I'm not packing rubber. Didn't think I'd need any." His hands settled on her rump. "You should've filled one of those crystal dishes full of them, set it right on the table with the chocolate fountain and aphrodisiac buffet."

"Not every lock-and-key connection ended in sex."

"Just the lucky ones, then?"

"You're saying that only because you're *getting* lucky." Light words, but if either of them were genuinely lucky, tonight would remain in clear perspective. Penetrative emotions wouldn't intersect with sex. She would give Santino Franco no more of herself than she'd given any other man. Except this time, she did it because she wanted the sex and nothing more. No ulterior motives. The new Bindi could sate her desires and not hurt anymore.

"My condoms are in the master suite. I'm tingly and lazy and *really* don't want to make that walk. I'm on the Pill and I'm clean."

"Okay."

"You believe me? I'm a liar." It wasn't something she'd highlight on a résumé, but until she changed it, she might as well own it.

"If a liar tells the truth, does that make her an honest woman? And…if an honest man tells a lie, does that make him a liar?"

That was a heavy question, and it provoked her to wonder whether good and bad weren't so distinct after all. "If you're going to ask philosophical questions, at least let me have a seat so I can really, carefully think this through." But the humor evaporated even before it had a chance to form. "What are you saying?"

"I'm saying I believe you."

She wanted to kiss him hard, except he stared at her so closely and his hands kneaded her booty so tenderly, she wasn't willing to interrupt. "What about you?"

"Clean—yes. Pill—no."

Bindi surrendered to a smile as she lowered onto him. "Oh, damn, Franco, don't be funny. I might start liking you, and then where would we be?"

What she didn't say was that it was already happening, and she was falling quickly into the most dangerous kind of trouble.

Bindi rode, stealing his control, so determined to take him higher and lure him deeper.

*Hold me…*

But he didn't. As a spasm seized him, he captured her hips in a tight grip and groaned as a series of hot spurts coated her.

"I'm freakin' lost in you." Jerking softly into her now, Santino held her face, tasted her lips. "You're so beautiful."

That word.

*Beautiful.*

As in *compliant.* As in *available.* As in *pleasing.*

"I'm going to take a shower." Peeling off her dress, she rose off Santino and pressed the expensive lace between her legs. "You might want to do the same."

He called her name, but she was already running to the staircase, running away, running so he wouldn't see her tears.

Soiled dress in the wastebasket, Bindi emerged from the en suite bathroom after a cold shower to light a fragrant oil and go to sleep.

She'd scrubbed herself clean, physically and emotionally, and could use a few hours of nothingness.

Abundant rain-spotted windows revealed a slightly tempestuous ocean shore and a sky that held an answerless darkness.

She'd come to the Seychelles for anonymity and escape, so how had she ended up having sex with Santino Franco, of all men—the *one* man on Cora Island who knew her sordid history?

Attraction. Greedy, destructive, inconvenient attraction.

Another weakness. Another flaw. And she'd managed to give into it again despite her goal not to.

What could she do now?

Bindi shoved open window after window. Tangy, almost masculine oceanic scents of salty air and sand burst into the bedroom.

Defying the rain-misted breeze, she raised her arms, closed her eyes and turned, twirled, spun. Reaching a point of dizziness where the bad didn't exist, she laughed, sank down and knew what she would do.

Get over it. She wouldn't let this mistake cancel her plans to better herself. She'd survive this misstep. Learned a good lesson. Would keep going for herself. And for no other reason than to make herself worthy of *her* love.

Finger combing her damp hair, she threw on undies

and her favorite comic-book-hero T-shirt and meandered out to the dim hall to test her eavesdropping ears. There was no angry piano music, but she detected noise from the billboard-size television downstairs.

Asleep, probably. Orgasms like the one he'd fired off could sap any man's energy, and he, more than most, needed the release. He had seemed so restless from the second she met his eyes in that crowded party.

How did he sleep? she wondered. Bare chested? On his side? With an arm flung over his eyes?

Each question brought her a footstep closer to the staircase.

"Forgot something?"

Bindi froze as arousal started melting her insides. Wet from a shower, Santino jogged up the stairs. In pants. Just pants. Great-fitting pants.

The horny-girl half of her brain instantly began devising strategies to remove them with her teeth. The other half prodded her to speak.

"I thought you'd be asleep."

"Naw. Considered it, but my mind kept trying to imagine you naked." Tugging something from his pocket, he said, "This didn't exactly help a brother out."

A thong.

*Her* thong.

"It's harassing me, not knowing what you look like," he said, tracing the thong over the design on her shirt.

Was she supposed to feel sorry for him? At least *he'd* come. She hadn't.

"Take this off." Venturing forward, he cased her in. "Let me have something to remember, not imagine."

*And let you call me "beautiful" again, when I'm anything but?*

"A look," he coaxed. "Just a look."

Sexual frustration peaked, and Bindi felt infused with…power. It intoxicated her, had her leading him to her suite. On her direction, he stood at the foot of her lavish bed.

She climbed onto the white-linen topped mattress, pranced to the headboard, faced the trio of framed coral reef prints.

Wind sighed against her skin as she drew the T-shirt over her head. "Just a look, you said." When he moved to one side of the bed, she skipped out of his reach. "What are you doing? A *look*, remember?"

"Now I want a kiss." He crossed to the other side fast—faster than she might've predicted possible. She dashed, barely avoided his grasp.

"Can't catch me? Can't kiss me," she taunted. Only when he returned to the end of the bed did she flounce her way back to the center of the headboard. "Mmm-mmm-mmm. I taste victory. It's delicious."

A heartbeat of silence, then he lunged, clasped her ankles and yanked hard. Her squeak dissolved in a peal of laughter as her backside hit perfumed linen with an impact that made the mattress quiver.

The laughter faded in their kiss. It demanded, threatened. Would their lives, their agendas, be intact when they left this bed?

*Get over it.*

Right. She'd be crazy to let the playful risk of this moment mean more than it should. Worse—let Santino mean more to her than he ever, *ever* should.

But the craziest thing she could do right now was deny herself the zing of pleasure that penetrated her as his beard grazed her.

Permission? He didn't request it. Warning? He deprived her of it.

Santino's mouth tantalized her breasts, sucked at their tips. "What's that you said about victory?"

"I—I—" A moan escaped. She was a moaner and had absolutely no chance of hiding it from this man. "I said…?"

"Mmm-hmm. Think."

With his teeth scraping her nipples? Not likely. "Can't."

"Yeah, you can."

*Breathe now. Nothing to fake here. Nothing to rush.*

"Oh… Victory's delicious."

Bringing her to the end of the bed, he spread her legs, then parted her folds with his tongue. "You're mine tonight," he said, so serious as he slid two large-knuckled fingers in deep.

The possessive, naked words, combined with the authority of his touch and the thoroughness of his mouth, pinned her still and baited her to recognize what turned her on…turned her inside out.

Her reaction to him was instinctual, as involuntary as a heartbeat. She clutched his head, but could neither push him away nor urge him closer. She wanted to watch, wanted to understand why a man who'd had so much taken away would be so giving. Only, pleasure pressured her to lie back, close her eyes and take—

Goose bumps rose on her arms and her nipples tightened as a breath of wind brushed her. "The windows! Shut the windows."

"Rain's stopped."

So it had. When, she had no clue. "Shut them anyway. I told you before, I don't perform for audiences." She'd already played a risky game, wrapping her legs around him on the veranda.

"Someone'd have to hover in a helicopter to sneak a peek," he reasoned.

"Someone might *hear* me."

"Hear you?" Only then did he take his mouth away. "Hear you scream, maybe? You're going to scream for me?"

"Not if all these windows stay open. It's up to you."

Santino's response was to kiss the inside of her thigh, abrade her skin with his beard and nip her to draw a sharp gasp. "Hot, Bindi, but that wasn't a scream. I'm going to get you to scream out these windows so the entire damn island knows you're being done right."

"*That* isn't gonna happen."

"No?"

"'Fraid not."

Then his hands were holding hers and her feet were pressing into his shoulders. She was shaking with need, but stuck in a battle of wills. Fighting him, she fought herself, too. Control or be controlled—she didn't know which to choose.

"I want the windows shut." *I think...*

He answered her demand with "I want my tongue in you when you come, but nod if you want me to stop. Nod for me, all right, and I'll stop right here and shut them. I'll take my time about it, make sure they're locked and everything's nice and secure and private."

What if this intensity couldn't be recaptured? Would he make her want and wait on purpose—play with her again?

"Or shake your head no if you don't want me to stop. Shake your head and ride out every moment of this." He kissed her intimately, and she might've hit the damn floor if he wasn't anchoring her to the bed. "Up to you."

When she shook her head, growled out the word *no*

maybe a dozen times for good measure, he grunted a laugh, then shattered her with the harshest orgasm she could remember.

Breaking for him, screaming because she couldn't resist, she let him hold her hands and hold her down as she let go.

After her slow writhing and quieting moans revealed the last of the sensations were coasting through her, she felt herself being freed.

Releasing her hands, striding across the room to the large windows, Santino said, "You wanted these closed, right?"

"Before I screamed myself hoarse, yes," she said, flipping onto her belly. The tingle on her thighs and V predicted whisker burn in her future. "So to get me to join you in the States, you're bribing me with the promise of revenge sex?"

"Fun revenge sex."

"Cute, Franco. But my decision stands. I'm not getting on a plane with you. Can't give up another week in paradise for fantastic sex."

"Fantastic sex *is* paradise. To some."

"To you?"

"Tabitha was paradise."

More like a mirage, but Bindi wasn't going to dwell on technicalities. "She's back in your head. I'm not mad about it."

Tabitha's footprints were all over this man—not that it came as much of a shock. According to Bindi's mother, who'd strived to be a perfect Christian wife to her perfectly imperfect husband, from Eve to Delilah to Jezebel, a woman's betrayal could leave some nasty damage.

She imagined love—the odd, complicated accessory it seemed to be—gave betrayal that extra something to make it slice deeper and hurt longer. Love, the same as fidelity and loyalty, were risks the men in her reality refused to let weaken their journeys to glittering success and enviable power.

"A person shouldn't be your paradise," she said.

"What we had going—ah, damn, it was so good. My life was good when we were solid like that. When she left, the good went with her."

"I think she left hot on the heels of all that good you're talking about. You were still in the NFL, the Slayers were still a Franco-owned team and Al was still a guy you could recognize as your father. When the tide turned, Tabitha turned." Not all that keen on keeping up a discussion about a woman whose ambitions had once mirrored her own, Bindi sighed deeply into the covers. "I ate an illegal amount of chocolate, did naughty things with you on a piano bench, let you do *very* naughty things to me on this bed and screamed sex noises out the windows. All that's left is for you to roll me up in these superfancy covers like a burrito and let me sleep through tomorrow."

*Or hold me. Be different.*

The others had never held her. They'd called her beautiful and sent a car for her. Or they'd passed out, spent, and left her to shower and book it before they awoke.

Santino's arm came around her, her back was to his front and she thought she might either cry because she so wanted to be held or freak out because this felt suspiciously like snuggling, and she wasn't supposed to be the kind to let her ex-fiancé's son snuggle her after a night of total-mistake sex.

She was the kind who ran like mad away from her mistakes.

"I— I'm not a…a, uh, cuddler." Stuttering, really? "What I mean is, we can stay like this for a few, but it's not something I do regularly." At least the words were out there. Awkward as all get-out, but out there.

"And I don't stay the night," he said, nuzzling her shoulder. "But…"

But he'd spent the night with her.

What were they doing? What were they thinking? What was wrong with them?

"I have a question."

*Add it to the pile, man.* "Yeah?"

"Why the Marvel shirt?"

She giggled. "Oh, that. My daddy went off the deep end for that sort of thing before I was born. Graphic novels. Comic books. He took me to ComicCon once, and we had the best time." She liked to pretend he'd been her loving father—and not a monster—then. "He bought me the shirt. Much too large, but who cares?"

"You got a thing for red capes or bat signals or webs?"

"Okay, I *did* find Batman pretty damn intriguing. When I decided to dress up as him for Halloween, my mom suggested I be Batgirl or, even more appropriate, Mrs. Batman."

"What'd you do?"

"Put on a Batman costume three Halloweens in a row."

His easy chuckle mingled with her giggles, and the blended sound was strange. They didn't laugh together. Tension and resentment had always taken up all the space between them.

"Anyway," she said after a while, "I was more into supernatural abilities than any specific superhero or supervillain. Not the standard flying ability or abnormal strength."

"I wouldn't be against telekinesis," he said. "What'd you want?"

"Invisibility. I wanted to be invisible." She slid her

eyes closed. "Before I matured and learned to be comfy in front of the camera—too comfy, if you want to count how many times I've ended up on somebody's gossip page—I dreamed about disappearing."

"From what?"

"My looks."

"You're beautiful. That beauty probably made your ride through life smoother than it could've been."

*Wrong!*

Though few would cop to it, wealthy men, influential men, men with discriminating tastes saw her "beauty" as merchandise. She knew because she'd cashed in on it far too many times.

Feeling dirty, she lifted his arm, rolled away from him and sat up. "You should get downstairs, give the sofa a chance. I'm going to shower—"

"Again?"

"Yes." Relieved when he went to the door without another word, she added, "First one awake fixes coffee."

"Bindi—"

"Good night, Santino."

"Good night."

She locked the door behind him. It had been one hell of a good night. Now she needed to figure out how to move on from her hottest mistake ever.

But first, a shower. And another cleansing cry.

## Chapter 5

Did roughly forty minutes of drifting, skulking on the rickety edges of awareness, count as sleep? Lying on a sofa that was a few inches too short to be accommodating, his eyes closed, Santino had remained vigilantly connected to his surroundings during that time and in the quiet, sluggish hours that followed.

He didn't know what he waited for, didn't legitimately expect his father to come banging on the door to do business with his ex. Had there been opportunities for Bindi to sneak a call to Al and warn him off? Damn straight. It was entirely possible for her to be in Santino's arms one minute, then on the phone with his father the next.

Almost every particle of him believed she'd somehow played a part of Al's disappearance. Suspicion had spread through him from corner to corner before getting here, so despite the glimpses of raw honesty he found in Bindi, he couldn't force himself to trust her—or anyone—completely. The world he lived in didn't allow it. But he wouldn't accuse her of organizing his father's escape from Las Vegas and enabling him to survive underground, because he didn't think her involvement ran that deep.

Because even she didn't know the role Al had assigned her.

A discreet, precisely planned and almost irresponsibly expensive vacation wasn't something a man—even one with a slipshod grasp on his *sanità mentale*—paid for and forgot about. Gambling debt must've already begun closing in on him at the time he'd taken Bindi as his fiancée. Yet he'd spent what must have been a hell of a supply of funds to make a two-week stay in this paradise possible.

Then he'd canceled the engagement, but not the trip. Why?

What was his gamble? What did he have to gain by approaching a woman he'd strung along in a tropical haven? Touring the Seychelles and entertaining strangers in the villa could eat up only so many hours, leaving dots of moments that were bound to find her alone— reimagining the villa's garden or kicking up sand on a beach or lagging behind a crowd on a Victoria street. Those moments of isolation were taken for granted, and what if that was what Al was banking on?

Because isolated, Bindi was integral, necessary to Al. Was she a throwaway key to freedom he didn't deserve? Or did he figure she owed him for the luxurious life she'd lived on his dime—and he was ready to collect?

That suggestion made Santino burn with an unfamiliar brand of anger that stretched inside him and settled.

As dawn breached the dark, he was glad to unfold himself off the sofa and fix the damn coffee. To be the first one awake, he would've had to *sleep* first. But he wasn't about to let his restlessness and a trivial technicality spark another go-around with Bindi.

Something infiltrated his strongest defenses when his temper met hers. It didn't stop and end with lust. If it did, he could cease the self-inflicted sweet torture of reliving the sight of her, the sound of her, her scent and touch and taste. Getting hot, getting hard and getting off didn't happen for him often—but it did happen, so that wasn't what made her exceptional. And it didn't make him cured. It was the intimacy she'd offered and he'd selfishly taken, as she rode him, came for him and let him hold her while she talked about superheroes, that got to him.

Damn, did she get to him—in ways that had nothing to do with his libido. If he never put a hand on her again, she'd still get past his barricades and occupy too much space in his head. Last night had been a mistake. Odds were it would happen again if they found themselves in another mistake-making mood. Self-restraint failed him, so yeah, let distance step in.

Santino had given her too much, and that fact made her reminiscent of Tabitha. But he'd taken just as much from Bindi, and he couldn't leave this island without taking one more thing: answers.

If she came close to satisfying his questions as completely as she satisfied his body, then ambushing her on this island wouldn't have entirely counteracted his purposes.

And those questions wouldn't be satisfied if he pissed her off about a pot of coffee.

Figuring out the futuristic-looking brewer was a distraction he appreciated. Leaning over a counter, mumbling a few curses, he got some relief from suspicion and erotic memories. On the other side of the windows lining one of the kitchen walls, an oasis-type terrace tried to lure him. Leafy plants swayed. Birds called out.

He poured a cup, drank down the steaming coffee without flinching. One of the worst moves he could make involved giving in to any temptation to hang around here when he knew he should leave. What he *should've* done was left Bindi alone last night—no unlocking her, no kiss, no sex, no wanting her with a ruthlessness that was as damaging as it was healing.

*Get out, Franco.* Walking away seemed easy enough. He'd make himself scarce, take a look around the island, send an "I'm alive, be cool" response to his brother's text messages. All better options than chillin' on Bindi's borrowed terrace, waiting for the smell of coffee to draw her out of her hiding place—no matter how much it killed him to wonder if she'd come stumbling half-awake straight to the brewer or waltz in bright eyed and on guard.

Either way she'd be hot as all hell.

With that realization echoing around his head, he got out of there, shoving his phone and wallet into his pockets and swinging open the front door.

A shard of a second too late he remembered the place was armed with a security system that would, if rigged with typical entry and glass-break sensors, fill the estate with ear-stabbing noise and send out a signal to authorities.

Except…nothing happened. A veranda decorated with rain-drowned tea-light candles and the peaceful whispers of the early morning greeted him.

A quick scan revealed no controls panel, but he didn't need to see it to confirm the system hadn't been activated. Being with him wasn't the only risk Bindi had taken last night.

*Step back. Don't start caring. Quit gambling what you can't afford to lose.*

As he made fast tracks for his rental truck at the edge of the property, Santino passed Villa Soleil's carport. A powder-blue convertible slept behind the wrought iron gates. The cool, calming color was starkly different from the sunshiny yellow of the Lamborghini he'd gotten used to finding parked in his driveway. Both vehicles were part of Bindi's illusions. She'd rented the convertible from the same Cora Island company that had provided his truck. The Lamborghini had sold well at an auction, and she'd bought a forgettable gray crossover that was easy to overlook on any Vegas street.

Almost invisible.

Invisibility—that was what she told him she'd wanted. Could be she wanted it again after what his father had put her through. Could be she'd find herself willing to make a devil's bargain to get what reality denied her.

Navigating the open island roads and allowing his periphery to take in clear waters and jungle-coated hills, he regretted that he'd even tried to bat away suspicion. Because now he prayed for it to catch hold again, choke out empathy and let him breathe.

At Cora Island Resort Hotel, he surveyed the concierge desk. A pair of men commanded the desk while a woman who'd stuffed her supersize breasts and hips into a dark suit spoke into a hands-free device and manipulated a tablet. When she set down the tablet and he could see a pair of gold crossed keys on her jacket lapel, he knew he'd wait for her.

The double shot of chipper he could do without, and he could easily get distracted picturing her rolling her hair around beer cans to come up with those cyclone-size curls, but Cecelia Whit had earned her Les Clefs d'Or keys after fifteen years in the industry, specializing in the delicate needs of politicians and high-profile celebrities. Her reputation as a woman who collected skeletons to keep the island's closets clean said she was as much of an enemy as she was an ally.

If his father roamed this island, she would know.

As he stepped forward, Cecelia sliced her hand

through the air and the men retreated to the opposite end of the glossy desk.

*"Bienvenue,"* she cooed. "Welcome to Cora Island Resort Hotel. I'm—"

"Cecelia Whit."

Cutting her spiel short, she said, "Follow me," and strode to an office behind the gatekeepers' desk. Coconut trees stood outside the windows, which he barely had time to notice, because she immediately snapped the blinds shut and gestured to a chair. "You read people, but I'm better at it. Age, if nothing else, has given me an edge. You were watching me because you have a special request, or you're fond of older women."

"Which do you think it is?"

"About your special request," she said. "Paranoia's making you hesitate. Am I correct?"

"Paranoia. Protecting my interests. Same thing."

"What can our resort do to earn your confidence?"

"I'm searching for somebody. Word is you like to think you run this island."

"I don't fool myself with delusions. This island is mine, sir. I've earned it and, yes, I do run it. Like a well-greased machine." Selling herself, she revealed her eagerness to add his skeletons to her collection. "You need more than discretion, don't you?"

"I need someone found." Santino laid a photo on the desk. "Would you recognize this man if you saw him?"

"The jaw. I would recognize the jaw. It's similar to yours." Eye fondling the photo, Cecelia asked, "Uncle?"

"Father."

"He's an Italian?"

"He is."

"Knew it. I have an eye for classic Italian men." Tossing her beer-can curls, she allowed a curt smile. "This man's not a guest here."

"At this resort?"

"On Cora. I keep track of visitors. The more peculiar, the more interesting. For instance, you arrived on Cora after our resort's posted check-in time, secured yourself a rental vehicle and neglected to claim any of the properties or attempt to book a room here—despite last night's weather conditions."

Half intrigued, half creeped out, he said nothing.

"A *very* interesting American tourist—attractive, young, curious—arrived by ferryboat last week. She's the biggest solo spender Cora's had the pleasure of accommodating in some time. Last night she hosted a Valentine's party."

"Were you there?"

"No," she said. "But *you* were."

"If I was? So?"

"Those are only observations."

"What do you make of your observations?"

"She provided your shelter. She's visited our resort for a cup of coffee at the top of every morning since she arrived on Cora Island. She neglected to join us this morning." An eyebrow rose. "I have a guess or two as to the explanation for that, but it's neither professional nor relevant to what you're asking of me."

Damn. Cecelia Whit was good—big hair, fancy crossed keys and all.

"Should we be expecting your father?" she asked.

"Look out for him as if you are. If he does arrive on this island, I need to know about it. Only me. Don't alert him. Don't drag authorities into this."

"Then, we'll call this a family matter, Mr. Franco?"

She knew his name. Of course she did. Within minutes

after he left her office she'd know who his father was and why Santino needed him found. "Yeah."

Another brisk smile. "Sir, I need to disclose that the safety of the resort's guests comes first. Keep that in mind when you decide how you'd like to proceed in re-connecting with your father, if he does join us on this island."

Agreeing on a nonrefundable two-thousand-euro gratuity—Cecelia's exclusive services might not guar-antee results, but her cooperation had its price—Santino gave her a contact number and left.

He didn't have a database of shady sentinels on the Seychelles, could trust no one, but with a set of eagle eyes secured on Cora Island, he felt better about going back to the States without Bindi Paxton.

The sun was higher in the sky, and his Bulgari chro-nograph watch read half past seven by the time he slowed his truck in front of Villa Soleil. Getting out, he heard Bindi say, "You should be halfway to Mahé by now."

Rounding a quartet of palm trees, she was neither sleepy-eyed and craving a coffee fix nor as prettied up as she'd been last night. In sunglasses, a baggy gray sweater, white bikini bottoms and sand sparkling on her bare feet, she was his biggest threat. Because he wanted to go to her, tug loose the side ties on her bikini pants and for-get why he'd be a supreme dumb ass to touch her again.

She carried a bottle of Guinness and a gigantic Fris-bee. Even a safe several feet away he could smell her: sunshine, sweat, sand...and—oh, damn, baby—fresh laundry.

"I fixed the coffee, Bindi."

"I know. I didn't drink any—I'd already decided on the Guinness. Um, I didn't expect you'd follow through on that."

"It was just coffee."

"Yeah. Thanks. Um…so…why are you here now? A morning-after gold star?"

"I can't leave without taking one more crack at you."

Her mouth opened, closed, opened again. "One more crack?"

"Questions," he clarified.

"*Questions?* Oh. Goody." The sarcasm couldn't mask the nervous anticipation she'd let slip a moment ago. "Ask me out back, on the beach. I was going balls out on my workout, till your noisy tank of a truck interrupted me."

"I didn't know it was possible to go balls out drinking beer and throwing around a big-assed Frisbee," he said, slowing to a stop just before the grass gave way completely to sand.

She handed him the beer, walked about another yard out toward the calm water, waved the disc. "Chasing this thing down, jumping to catch it, bending to pick it up—all excellent cardio. Plus, since it rained overnight, the sand's mushy and makes for some great resistance, which is awesome for strength endurance."

"And you keep hydrated with beer?"

"It *is* a vacation." She lifted the disc, sent it zipping through the air and raced after it, kicking up breaths of sand with each step. "My mother said a lady breaks out the booze after noon, and a lush does it before noon."

"You believe that?"

"No. Anyway, the way I see it, noon has come and gone somewhere in this world." She jumped, snagging the disc and facing the reverse direction. "I don't know when your flight takes off, but you shouldn't let me keep you. Your questions?"

"So you booked all your reservations in advance. Fine, that makes sense. Who's paying for your extras, Bindi?

Morning coffees at the resort, sightseeing trips, souvenir shopping? Who footed the bill for the party?"

She paused, scowled. "Those are some personal questions."

"We had sex. How much more personal can we get?" He watched her leg muscles tauten and relax as she ran after the disc, then she bent to snatch it up when it suddenly flipped and dropped into the sand.

*You touched that before. You had that already. It's over.*

"Answer me," he hollered across the distance. "Answer me, then I'm gone. But don't lie to me."

"Al made sure I planned carefully."

She was holding something back and wasn't doing a decent job of hiding it. "Planned? Or schemed?"

"What does that mean?"

"It means there's more to this, and if you don't already know what that might be, you need to work with me—not against me."

"Really? So we'd be partners in this? Ride or die?" She laughed. *"Riiight."*

"I'll look out for you." Santino hadn't thought far ahead, hadn't come here to offer his protection to Bindi. But if she needed it—needed him—could he turn her down? "I mean that."

"No, thanks." She turned the disc in her hands, but didn't release it. "Al gave me funds for a spending allowance out here. I was bitter, feeling epically pissed and I splurged on the party and island hopping and it felt good."

"Is he authorized on the account?"

"No."

"Is it gone?"

"Chocolate fountain, top-trained serving staff, silver necklaces—it all adds up. There ought to be enough left to fund my excursion to see a hundred-year-old tortoise and some gift shopping."

Yeah, he could see her venturing off after tortoises and getting lost in racks of novelty stuff. That was a dimension of her he rarely saw in Las Vegas but knew existed.

But again, she was keeping her cards close to the chest.

"Is this about the money?" she asked.

"No, it's about motives. My father's. Yours. Mine, too." He switched the warm beer from one hand to the other. "Dammit. Why am I doing this? I should be in Vegas with my mind on the NFL."

"What?"

"Forget it." He'd retired from the league, but his jersey number hadn't been retired, and in his sport, comebacks could mean everything. A comeback, a dignified retirement on his terms—he was owed that, and if he defied science and the league welcomed him home, he would collect. "I'm doing everything to find my father. I'm trying to get to him, trying to get it through his head that running's going to make it worse. I'm the only man on this side of the fight, Bindi. My brother's in Las Vegas. He's smart. His hands are clean. Why am I doing this?"

"You love your father. You feel responsible for him."

"I shouldn't. I should hate him." He and his brother had promised their mother that they'd look after him, and every day Santino had to face what he'd lost because of his father, he found it harder to honor that promise.

"But you can't hate him. The Alessandro Franco I know isn't the one you know. He's your father, and once, before I met him, he was a good man." Bindi raised the disc, settled into her stance. "Hating him now would sure make crap easier, but that's not an option you have. You know the other sides of him. And because of that you can't hate him."

When she threw the disc, it floated levelly at first, then it suddenly changed course and, wobbling, veered in his direction. She yelled, "I got it!" as he reached for it, and before he could register that she was charging toward him, they met in a dull collision with her head striking his chin and the disc ending up in his hand anyway.

The real tragedy was the beer bottle tipping and a stream baptizing the sand.

Grabbing his hand to right the bottle, she said, "Either my scalp's bleeding or by sunset I'm going to have one of those cartoon lumps."

"Want me to check it out?" He was already dropping the monster Frisbee and reaching for the spot on her crown that must've ached like a bastard.

"It's all right." She refused, taking the beer and a greedy swig of it. "Nice catch, though. Here, have a sip."

He didn't always go for warm beer, but Santino couldn't refuse the sweet gesture. She did that a lot—shared. She was self-serving, had an on-again, off-again relationship with honesty, but she shared what she had. Her generosity was as hot as anything about her.

Passing the beer back, he said, "Let's give that no-lying thing another try. Tell me…how come you've got nothing underneath this sweater?"

Bindi's gaze landed on him like an openhanded slap. "I—"

"Okay, let's clear up something. Before you get the urge to say you've got on a bra or whatever." With both hands free, and his decent judgment running on empty, he tucked them under the bottom of the sweater and slid them up her sweat-dampened abdomen to cover her breasts. "I wasn't asking *if* you were naked under this," he said, scraping his thumbs across her stiff nipples. "I was asking why."

"I—I—" She made an ineffective one-handed attempt to slow him down. "I was going to work on a tan. An all-over tan."

*Get to it*, he almost said. *Show me.*

"Santino, what'd you think was going to happen when you found me here?"

"You'd hear me out, pack up your purple luggage and go back to Vegas with me."

"Who said I have purple luggage?" She stumbled backward.

Shit, he wasn't going to admit to hanging on to a file devoted to her secrets. "It's a guess. Your Frisbee's purple."

Bindi nodded slightly. "Okay. Good luck with the whole Al situation."

She was distancing herself. He didn't like it but had to let it happen. "Call me if—"

"Definitely. And you have my number?"

"Memorized."

"Better be." Her smile seemed forced. "Go. I have a workout to finish, a possible concussion and who knows what else?"

"Concussion? Without a possible concussion you forgot to activate the security system on this place, by the way. What are you going to do with your bell rung?"

"Wait. I activated the system last night. I told you I left the terrace entry inactive for your benefit."

"I left through the front door."

Bindi frowned again, glanced toward the villa. "Then, I must've forgotten after all. So my secret's out—I'm human and capable of errors."

"I'm not leaving you alone with a possible concussion."

"First, my head's fine. It was just a little lighthearted sarcasm. Second, I won't be alone."

"Are you going to get your chance with that man at the party? The one with the 'fro and piercings?"

"Might," she said, and he knew she wasn't lying. "I could get with him, if the stars lined up just right. We're not exclusive, Franco. We're not…anything."

He nodded because she was right, not because he agreed. He nodded even though he probably would've crushed the Guinness bottle in his hand if he'd still been holding it.

"Take care." Before he could turn his back, Bindi yanked off her sweater and gave him a teasing, unobstructed view of her jogging nearly naked with her oversize Frisbee and the bottle of beer they'd shared.

Bindi stayed outside—her heart beating too fast, the sun too hot on her skin—and counted Mississippis until she heard Santino's truck drive away from her villa. When it did, at three hundred and sixteen Mississippi, she dropped her disc, grabbed her sweater and ran inside.

Getting rid of the beer bottle, she ran faster, clumsier, to the front of the house. Hidden behind one of the black-and-white prints beside the door was the security system's control panel. She moved the decoy, studied the panel.

Inactive.

She'd set the system to Active as surely as she locked all seven locks on her Vegas apartment door and made sure her Louisville slugger was where it should be.

Someone had deactivated it.

Chilled, as though someone had scraped a feather down her spine, Bindi rushed to put on her sweater.

She bolted upstairs to the master suite, grabbing the closet key she'd hidden from prying guests. Opening the door with shaking hands, she stared at her Louis Vuitton suitcases. Santino had said with a lot of freaking certainty that her luggage was purple.

How had he known if she'd kept it hidden? He hadn't looked inside her closet.

"You're having me tailed, Franco."

Rage kissed her quietly, caressed her comfortingly, coaxed her to embrace it. Because she wasn't only angry—she was hurt that he would lie to her and deceive her even as he volunteered to "look out" for her.

*This* was why she withheld. *This* was why she was right to quit trusting a man's word.

This was why she had to sink to their level to ensure she'd come out on top.

Bindi blotted her eyes and grabbed her phone. In Las Vegas, the newspaper editor in chief who was sexual harassment defined and had refused to interview Bindi for a reporter gig because she'd refused him, was probably in the middle of a Valentine's Day dinner with his wife, but she knew he'd take her call.

"Drew Ross. Go," he said when he answered.

Bindi cringed. She despised every smarmy thing about this man, but despised even more that she was backsliding into sleaze. Perhaps things truly did have to get worse before they could get better. "This is Bindi Paxton."

"We don't have business," he said, hostile.

"I want a job."

"I think you're aware of the effort I need you to show first," Drew said, in a way that tempted her to pitch her phone out the window.

"I'm aware. And I won't do that."

"Then don't contact me—"

"You're going to want to hire me when I give you exclusive updates on Alessandro Franco."

"Alessandro Franco skipped town."

"His son wants me to help him find Alessandro. I just decided I'm going to do it." It was too unfair for Santino to screw her literally and figuratively. She wanted to use, instead of be used yet again. "It's only a matter of which media entity gets the details as they happen."

"Santino Franco shut out the media."

"Not me. Give me a job, Ross. Salaried, with benefits."

"Jumping the gun, aren't we? Get me something substantial on the papa and the godpapa. Gian DiGorgio's in the vortex, too."

Gian DiGorgio triggered fear she never could describe, like an itch that was too deep to scratch. Mostly, she'd stayed out of his way. But when she couldn't avoid him, she'd laughed at his jokes, let him leer a little when Al wasn't paying too much attention and reminded him often that her fidelity was to the man who'd put the ring on her finger.

"I'll get what I get," she said, stressing that she controlled the terms, trying to downplay the desperation she tasted on her own lips. "Franco, DiGorgio, the Las Vegas Slayers, gambling and football. You want in on that action, Ross."

"Come to my office and let's chat about the job."

"No, a public place, and I'll decide when. To be clear, you'll never come on to me again. A salaried position at the paper and some respect are all I want."

An hour later, she was composed and dressed up, on Mahé and flat broke. A visit to the bank that held her allowance account confirmed that close to half a million euros remained available even after the efforts she'd made to mindlessly spend it all. So she drained the account, taking none for herself but anonymously donating the funds to a Seychelles conservation society.

Santino's questions about the money for her "extras" had made her rethink why Al had given her so much money to play with when she was reserving the vacation. They hadn't set a wedding date, for hell's sake, yet he'd had her starry-eyed about a Valentine's Day trip.

It was strange, and since she had no intention of taking the funds to the US, she spent absolutely everything here.

Now, as she stopped in front of an internet café, she wished she'd brought along enough for a cup of coffee. She'd skipped coffee at Cora Island's gorgeous hotel, hadn't even sampled what Santino had fixed hours ago.

But she had an idea.

Santino didn't answer her call with a regular "Hello" or "Hi." He said her name, and his voice was as boldly intimate as his hands had been on her body earlier.

"I realized, since I didn't drink the coffee you brewed this morning, you still owe me," she said into the phone, half wondering if anyone on the busy street was there to stalk her.

"Where are you?"

"Mahé. In front of a café."

"Bindi… You changed your mind about coming with me?"

"Yes. But I could change it again, if you don't get me that coffee quickly enough."

"You didn't give up your second week in paradise for a damn cup of coffee. You know you're doing the right thing."

Betraying him to suit her purposes because he'd betrayed her to satisfy his agenda was the right thing? It didn't feel right. It felt dirty, but then again, shouldn't she be most familiar with that?

"Santino…" She wanted to backpedal, right here on the street. She wanted to scream into the phone that she did hate him, because he'd hurt her when she'd thought she couldn't be hurt again.

"I knew you'd come through for me."

"You won't always be able to predict me," she warned, because she felt she had to warn him that the landscape of their game had changed.

"I'm not always going to want to predict you." He said it like a promise. Promises were usually preludes to lies. But when he added, "I'm going to protect you, Bindi," she closed her eyes.

Because he said it as though he meant it, as though he knew how much she wanted to believe it and how much it hurt to know she couldn't take that risk.

Alessandro didn't recognize himself. In a square, musty bathroom above his nemesis's ceramics market, as good as hidden in a fishing village in Sicily, he could peer through the thick, cracked mirror and see a sixty-four-year-old defying his age with an at-home dyeing kit that darkened his hair and whiskers to "natural black" when not so long ago he'd been smooth jawed, with his silver-gray hair expensively trimmed.

He could still see the ghosts of his past, though. No makeover could hide them when he looked at his reflection. A gap-toothed runt of a child, a second-generation Italian immigrant, playing barefoot and scrape kneed and innocent in a relative's lemon orchard. A gawky teenager with odds stacked in his favor and aces up his sleeves, eager to make America his permanent home and guard with his life the Francos' prosperous eyewear company's Nevada arm. A young man, slick with success, already hardened by corporate logistics, constructing alliances with giants among men and climbing to his success on the backs of others. A husband, a prisoner in love's bondage, figuring out that growing his fortune like corn in a field with his family's wealth and his ownership of Las Vegas's only professional football franchise wasn't as essential as his Gloria.

A father. Fatherhood was a privilege, and he'd spat on it. The boys were his first wife's most treasured legacy. He'd destroyed each of his strong, warrior-like sons. His eldest son had grown up to share Alessandro's love for football, had been a star in the NFL until he'd had to pull his star from the sky and throw him into the depths. His other son had betrayed him, as many sons betrayed their fathers: for the sake of a woman.

*Bella* Charlotte Blue. Al appreciated the look of the woman who'd won his younger son's loyalty. A stunning, curly-haired African-American beauty, she reminded him of Gloria.

*"Cazzo."*

Al shut his bloodshot, rheumy eyes, skated a hand over the whiskers that didn't do much to camouflage his hollowed-out cheeks and the jagged angles of his bony face.

He had been handsome once. When Gloria had died, he'd worn her death, reflected it. The details about her— the color she liked on her nails, the habits that had annoyed him, who she included in her nightly Christian prayers—he'd started to forget soon after he'd lost her. But her essence and her aura stayed with him, even when he'd remarried twice and set out to marry again.

Marrying Daisy, a fashion-magazine somebody, and Penelope, a teacher who'd been so confident that she'd hit the jackpot that she'd retired the week of their wedding, he had felt Gloria's anger. Proposing to Bindi, a young woman with the kind of wisdom you didn't get living a safe, protected life, he'd felt Gloria's grief. There was nothing he could do for Bindi except hurt her—he'd know that when he'd promised to take care of her.

Her beauty was so addictive, her spirit purer than even she recognized. Bindi had denied him, and when he'd finally lost his sons' respect, his reputation and his maybe even his mind, too, he thought he had lost his chances of making her his. But he would get her back.

Gian DiGorgio, his comrade, his only prayer of living as a free man, had helped him slip out of the United States and travel unseen to Italy. Friends took care of each other, so Al knew he could trust Gian's promises. After all, without Al's assistance, Gian wouldn't have been able to make over a billion dollars of side cash betting on games. Al had come through for the man. Now it was Gian's turn to come through for him.

Al touched his damp hair, trying to get used to the new look. When was the last time he'd had a head full of purely dark hair? Decades ago, it had to be. He'd started graying in his thirties. His son Santino, a good-looking boy, was beginning to gray with a few silvery streaks at the sides.

"My son. My boy." Al sighed, stepped back from the mirror. He'd never see either of his children again, but that was something he'd accepted when Gian had come to him with a way out. At least he'd have a woman to make the days a little more bearable.

Tonio, whose ancestors had been mortal enemies to Al's ancestors, whose father and long ago fallen out of favor with Al's father when a business investment had turned out to be as valueless as a week-old cannoli, had come to him a few days ago with word that Bindi Paxton had made her way to the Seychelles.

Not even Bindi could piss away over two million dollars, so he had not a worry that she'd spend the money he needed to survive. Tonio, who was ten years out of prison, had given up narcotics and had said up front that he could hold Al only so many days—as a favor to Gian. So the sooner Al could get to the Seychelles and coerce his gorgeous ex-fiancée to open the treasures that belonged to him—first the bank account that held his funds, next that beautiful body of hers—the sooner he could begin again.

This time, he thought as he took the soft, creaky steps of a narrow stairwell down to the kitchenette of Tonio's market, he'd live a humble life. Perhaps he'd run a market of his own, or buy his own lemon orchard. As an afterthought, he considered Bindi. She could adapt, if she wanted his money desperately enough. Or, if need be, he'd take the money from her and they'd nicely part ways. She was intelligent, crafty, and would be smart enough to not cause trouble for him or Gian or anyone else who needed Al to make a safe, calm escape.

Potent scents of breads and sauce and spices, combined with the raucous clatter of violence, blessed the kitchenette. Al lingered on the final step, assessing the brawl in front of him. Despite his potbelly, Tonio had his fists wedged into the back of another man—kidney shots. On closer inspection, Al found the dull, dingy floor streaked not with sauce, but blood.

Grunting, Tonio's victim scrambled for a broom.

To earn his keep, Al had to interfere. He crossed the room fast, skidding on a puddle of blood, and kicked the broom out of the man's reach.

Tonio landed a few final battering strikes, then kicked the man and gave a labored laugh as the man slid and hit a stool. *"Figlio di puttana!"*

The man coughed, struggled to his feet.

"He stole from me," Tonio said to Al, pulling a dented package of smokes from a pocket. Offering one, he nodded his thanks. "Nobody steals from me. Eh, I'm a teddy bear of a guy, right? I let him walk. He's walking away."

Al said nothing, but watched as the man slumped over a counter and struggled to lift his dark head.

"Be back here in an hour to work," Tonio shouted to the man as he limped out the scratched wooden door. "They don't make good help these days, do they, Franco?" Another labored laugh, this one whistling with congestion and Al wasn't surprised. Tonio was in advanced stages of congestive heart failure.

"Franco, I got through the channels some information you're going to need."

Al searched Tonio's faded brown eyes. "Go on."

"That *bella donna* you're going out to the Seychelles for? She ain't there."

"Bindi Paxton. It's a two-week vacation. Of course she's still there."

"She ain't there," Tonio repeated coldly. "She left."

Why would Bindi leave in the middle of an all-expenses-paid vacation? Had Gian relocated her? Had someone warned her that Al was coming for her?

"Gian will be connecting. Give him time. But Franco, this ain't a permanent arrangement. Track down the *bella donna* and do it fast." Tonio tsked, went to grab a dishcloth. "Look at this. Cut knuckle. But a man fights with his God-given weapons."

Al's mind felt light, fragmented. If Bindi was gone, how would he access the money stored in her account? How would he begin again without the woman he needed? "There's no shame in fighting with manmade weapons," he said to Tonio.

"No," Tonio agreed after a hollow moment. "But there's no pride in it, either."

## Chapter 6

Bindi took a moment to center herself—the way she'd been taught in the Acting 101 course she'd signed up for freshman year when she'd had bright ideas about finding herself and veering off her parents' journalism- and law-focused paths in a pursuit of happiness—before sashaying into the only establishment in Las Vegas she considered a true-blue friend.

Cleopatra's Barge wasn't the epitome of glamor, wasn't the most exclusive lounge in this city and yes, some were intimidated by the floating craft's unique, proudly wanton breast-baring statues that provocatively greeted you at the entrance, but for her it was something she could depend on when she wanted an extra shot of confidence or pizzazz. The place had a personality that meshed with Bindi's, and without judgment or chastisement, it welcomed her into its warm hospitality.

Patrons probably didn't see past the red-and-gold decor, dance space, live bands and the prices of the drinks at the bar, but Bindi sort of enjoyed figuring out the soul of a place. More than a building or a gimmicky tourist haunt, the Barge was a friend. Bindi knew, because when her wolf of an ex-fiancé had begun to shed his sheep's clothing and she'd dropped soundlessly out of Vegas society's favor, she'd watched her friends trot one by one out of her life, until there was just this club left to hold her up. It hadn't changed its attitude or appearance. It hadn't turned her away like a rat seeking shelter from the cold.

Maybe she was searching for hope in the wrong places, but she needed all the confidence she could find to get through tonight's meeting with Drew Ross. *The Vegas Beat* maintained a rivalry with the *Las Vegas Sun*, competing for readership and relevance in a technology-dependent world. The editor in chief had Hollywood-star charm and hunted news as though he were a predator beyond all redemption, and Bindi knew the extremes he'd take to gain an edge or get what he wanted.

She'd stuck to her guns when she'd contacted him to schedule a talk. No, she wouldn't come to his office when most of the staffers would be gone for the night. No, she wouldn't give him her address and let him bring over Chinese food. No, she wouldn't meet him in anyone's VIP room.

A public place, with people around, and where—God willing—a man and woman sitting down and talking business wouldn't be misconstrued as a serial gold digger looking for her next conquest.

Drew had at one point threatened to call off the deal, but when Bindi had calmly replied that she could accept his decision, he'd tried to steamroll her again. Now as she entered the club and looked through the strands of patrons moving about, she felt icky. She'd be nothing but professional tonight—would shake Drew's hand if he offered it and would be as transparent as any solid journalist strived to be. But it was the sleaziness of her knee-jerk reflex to make a side alliance with this man that she second-guessed.

An entire day after parting ways with Santino at Mc-Carran International, she was still raw from his duplicity. She was torn straight down the middle, half of her so livid that the shock of it made her catch her breath and the other half so unwound from being with him on the island that she imagined her skin tingling everywhere his mouth had touched her.

She'd had a clear goal when she had stepped off the ferryboat on Cora Island: get her crap together. With a kiss and a touch and a night of sex she couldn't erase, he'd unwrapped her ambitions and undone her progress. And by lying to her, taking away what she'd appreciated most about him, he'd shaken loose her respect. He hadn't tossed her taxi fare, swatted her ass and sent her on her way, but he'd damaged some piece of her all the same.

Or, he *would*, she reminded herself, if she didn't go through with her gut reaction to turn the tables. Sex was sex, but now they were dealing with survival. Journalism was the only career that might take in a disgraced politician's daughter who hadn't finished her college degree and had spent ten years prancing from one rich boomer to the next. It was the only industry that might pay her bills, even as it constantly held up a cruelly revealing mirror every time she pursued someone else's hardship.

She couldn't say she wanted this life any more than she wanted to give up her body and affection and future to men like Alessandro Franco. She'd prefer to someday look at her reflection and recognize someone she loved. She'd prefer to look at a man who loved her for her flaws, because her ugliness was as vital as her beauty.

A dream, though. It was just a dream.

Fully awake now, Bindi found Drew at the bar and prepared herself to do business.

Hollywood charm in position and his enormous ego no doubt polished by his inclusion in a BET television Black History Month feature on America's übersuccessful black urban men, Drew slid off his stool and took her hand as she approached. "Bindi Paxton, you're trying to kill me. Where you been? I'm liking the mocha skin and the dark hair... Mmm, girl."

"Drew, hello."

"All right, level with me."

"About?"

"What are you?"

Bindi paused. What was she? "A human being. A woman..."

Drew rolled his lips in a way that made her feel naked, and she didn't like it. His eyes half-mast, he said, "You got a white girl face, but a black girl booty."

Instant wrath nearly blinded her. Insulted, offended, she felt herself trembling. "Does it threaten you, to not know what I 'am'?"

"Not at all. I'm just curious about your recipe."

*Recipe?* What the actual— "Drew, I'm the product of people being free to travel this world and courageous enough to not let skin color or religion be an obstacle." Eventually those factors had come into play to sway her father to identify himself as African-American and to influence her mother to convert to her husband's religion to "simplify" their family. "And I prefer *genealogy*, not recipe. I'm not a damn soup."

There went her resolve to be utterly professional.

"Ease up now," Drew said, his gaze dropping low then riding up her body to her "white girl face." Likely he wished she'd do a twirl to show him her "black girl booty."

"I didn't mean any negativity. You'd do yourself a favor to not be so sensitive, if you want to work with me."

She didn't want to work with him, per se. She wanted a steady paycheck with benefits and some stability and a chance to contribute to society. High society shut her out, to be sure, but she was still a part of a social web, and she found it only fair that she pay it forward in some meaningful fashion. Donating the excess funds from an extravagant vacation was one thing. But suppose she were to find herself more involved in environmental conservation, in horticulture and rebirth and renewal and all the hopeful second-chance things that some believed nature symbolized?

If enduring the likes of Drew Ross led to that path, could she be courageous enough to crawl past adversity to find her way? Did she have to make more mistakes to make lasting changes?

"Drew Ross, I won't tolerate sexism or racism or anti-Semitism or any other filth you might be comfortable spewing at the *Beat*. I'll sue you if I have to. I will offer my services elsewhere if you have a gripe about that."

"I said ease up. It's not like that. C'mon, take this stool."

She sat beside him to find a clear drink waiting.

"Vodka all right with you?" he asked, reclaiming his stool and swiveling to face her fully. His tapered low-cut hair exposed three-sixty waves that were probably further emphasized by a pomade, and his brown eyes glittered. He reeked of cinnamon-flavored cigarettes, and on closer inspection his jaws jumped about every second and a half. He was chewing cinnamon gum to disguise the cigarette odor.

"I don't mind vodka," Bindi said as she flagged a bartender. "But I'd rather have a beer, please. Whatever's good on tap." One glass of vodka would hit her faster than three beers, and she wouldn't put it past Take-Initiative Drew to have banked on that.

"That was a freebie," Drew protested, raising a hand to ward off the bartender. "Take your drink, Bindi."

"No, thank you." She opened her purse, shuffled through a few checkout-lane gadgety trinkets, slid her fingers across her smartphone and grabbed her wallet. Thanks to her video recording of a prime-time drama sweetheart's tirade at a Reno shopping plaza last month, she could afford to buy herself a beer—and pay Drew for a drink she hadn't ordered. "Let me reimburse you for the vodka, Drew. The last thing I want is to start this professional relationship indebted to you."

Drew cursed, turned up the ginger-colored contents of his glass. "Forget it. Business expense. I'll write it off."

"My refreshments aren't your business expenses," she said after the bartender delivered the beer. "We're not in business together yet. That's why we're here—to establish some boundaries and rethink any unrealistic expectations either of us might have."

"Unrealistic expectations?" Drew suddenly clamped a hand down on one of her knees. "You won't be strutting yourself in my face dressed like this and thinking I'm not going to notice. That's an unrealistic expectation."

Bindi shook her head, confused. She was wearing a gauzy black sweater and metallic gold jeggings. Not a power suit, but not lingerie and a bow tie, either. And so what if she had been dressed down? It didn't give him the right to put his hand on her. "Off. Get the hand off. Now."

He did, though not before squeezing her kneecap harshly. "That's your problem. You've been with men from a different generation. They don't operate the way I do."

"Bullies come in all different ages, Drew. Did you enjoy holding on to me like you did a second ago? Because it's going to have to last you. Don't touch me again."

"I will."

"No."

"You don't say no," he objected, grinning. "All you know is *yes*. That's what you're going to be saying when we take this little discussion out to my car and we get those shiny pants off."

"No," she said again firmly. She was wearing crotch-stomping boots tonight, but wouldn't call on them. She had something else that'd change Drew's mind. "All these people here don't want to have their dancing ruined by security guards coming through to show you out."

"Security? They'd believe someone like you?"

"Eh…" She tipped her head to one side, then the other. "I'd like to think so, since my phone's been recording this conversation from the moment you tried to force that vodka on me. And I'm thinking security cameras got a great look at you grabbing me. By the way, I really hope you don't try that again, because next time I will go for the nuts and won't let up until they look more like raisins."

"Bitch."

"If by 'bitch,' you mean a clever and perceptive woman who gets things done, then, thanks." She took a careful swallow of her beer, a toast to her guardian half-nude statue. "Can we discuss business now? I do have other engagements."

"Other men to hunt?"

"I'm not searching for a relationship now, if that's what you're asking."

"Alessandro Franco scared you celibate?"

"Yes," she said, smirking so that he couldn't tell whether she was slyly joking or confessing the truth. If no one counted the no-boundaries night she'd shared with Santino, then yes, she was celibate. And it wasn't as though she cared that she rested on the shelf. The shelf was safe. For her, sex had never been designed for her pleasure. No man had worked hard to take her up high then let her tumble into the kind of ecstasy that made a woman sweat and scream.

*Scream.*

Bindi set down her bottle, blinked quickly. Her imagination shook apart, conjuring pictures of her naked with damp hair, sweat-misted skin and an irresistible devil of a man dining on every sensitive spot on her body.

Recalling every spectacularly dirty maneuver, she felt her toes curl in her boots and her fingers flex as though she could feel his taut flesh, and she thought for a simply silly moment that Santino Franco was designed for her pleasure.

Was she designed for his? Of course she wasn't. He'd said that his ex-girlfriend Tabitha had been his paradise. Paradise would be a tough act to follow, especially for a woman who had the trust capacity of a neglected and abused animal.

For that matter, what was she doing to even consider this? She and Santino had a one-night island fling, and on the island was where the details and the memories should stay. There'd been no mile-highing on the flights back to Las Vegas, no getting laid during the layover.

Only a solemn sense of unresolved tension that neither of them had—or would—explore now that they were in Sin City and partnering up to see to it that his father answered for his sins.

And Santino had double-crossed her. She couldn't forget that. She couldn't let that fury slip, because the man was swift and knew to target her weaknesses.

"I want to know why Alessandro Franco's golden boy would enlist you," Drew said flatly.

Santino was as far from a "golden boy" as anyone, she thought. No golden boy would hold her down on a fluffy mattress and use his tongue to—

"Uh—uh—" she stuttered, bringing her beer back into close range. She took a swallow. Nope, didn't work. Her body was still set on five-alarm arousal. "Santino thinks his father wants to find me. He believes I have something Al wants."

*"You?"* Drew snorted. "Criminals can be as dumb as rocks, but would a man who ran a billion-dollar gambling ring in this city risk getting caught for you? Doesn't make sense. I wouldn't do it."

"Good to know that should you find yourself facing criminal charges you won't be coming to me to save you."

"What does Santino plan to do when he gets hold of his father?"

"Turn him in."

Drew frowned. "He'd hand his father—and his god-father, Gian effin' DiGorgio—over to the feds? Not in a million years. Not with all that money at stake. Santino's got his own fortune, granted, but the Las Vegas Slayers was a billion-dollar franchise that his father sold for cheap. Where are the Slayers now? Damn Disney World." He laughed. "They've got championship rings. Marshall Blue and his wife performed a miracle. They took a scoop of dirt and turned it into gold. They're the ones raking in all that money, all the publicity. And Santino's supposed to be all right about it? Hell no, but I'm going see what information you give me. I want weekly updates. That's nonnegotiable."

"You called him a golden boy. Why would it be surprising that he'd have Al shake hands with justice?"

"Hey, now. I said he was a golden boy. I never said golden boys were stupid," Drew said, getting off his stool, holding up one hand and signaling for a fresh brandy with the other. "We're through here."

Released, Bindi grabbed her purse, turned off the recorder on her phone and went into the restroom to freshen her makeup. A quick stop to the apartment, and then she'd be on the road again, headed to Los Angeles. The bloggers she reported to had received a tip that a pair of rival hip-hop artists would be at an after-midnight club on Las Palmas. They'd contacted her, which was a rare event even though she had several months' seniority with their team. If she successfully made it into the club and walked out with enough pictures and videos to satisfy the team, she'd be able to not only pay the bills, but store a little away in her neglected savings account. One couldn't live off the sale of a luxury car alone. Beyond that, payday had this way of making her feel accomplished.

"So you finally figured out brunettes have more fun," a lilting feminine voice said.

Bindi turned away from the mirror with her lipstick uncapped. "Toya. What are you doing at the Barge?"

Toya Messa shook out her coil curls, fluffed her hair and eyed Bindi through naturally lush lashes. The no-mascara-necessary lashes, prominent cheekbones and flawless, consistently toasty skin tone had always provoked Bindi's envy. "Getting my dance on."

"You don't dance," Bindi pointed out, applying the lipstick with an expert hand. She'd been wearing makeup since age ten, and could probably apply a full face with her eyes closed. "At your wedding reception, you rocked in Asher's arms but didn't move your feet."

"Oh, I'm sure that was just my feet trying to warn me to turn and run from the courtyard," Toya said drily. She'd been a stunning April bride that year, barely out of college and joined in holy matrimony to Asher Messa of Messa Technologies. "Did it rain that day?"

"No, clear skies during the ceremony and a starry night canopying the reception." It'd been a fairy-tale kind of day. Perfect wedding, imperfect wedding. It made sense in a twisted way. "Why do you think it rained?"

"It would've been appropriate, had it rained." Toya shrugged. Not exactly petite, but almost shallowly thin, she didn't appear capable of holding much on those delicate shoulders. Which made it heartbreaking that she was a few months divorced and a single mom on top of it. News of Toya's divorce, and an estimate of what she'd stood to gain in the settlement, had come directly as Bindi's prospects were slipping away. Toya had slipped away from whatever impersonation of a friendship they'd shared then, and Bindi had let herself wallow in moments of despair because unlike Toya, she wasn't under twenty-five and college educated and it all had seemed so unfair.

Today, she could look through the mirror at the woman she'd wanted to be her friend and smile with humanity. "You don't like the rain, Toya. It makes you have wild hair. You used to call it Cray-Cray Kinky."

"I still call it that."

"Oh." Bindi capped the lipstick. "I didn't want to assume. I don't really know what's changed since your divorce and my broken engagement." Their friendship had unwoven then, and neither had made efforts to repair the damage.

"We could have coffee, catch up." Toya hastened to add, "Holden's off the boob now. I'm coffee approved."

"Holden. You had a boy?"

"He just turned six months." Consulting the mirror, she seemed bewildered with the image of herself that confronted her. "I had divorce papers in my purse the morning my water broke and I gave birth. The purse fell on the floor and there went the papers."

"I'm sor— Well, that's messed up."

"That's *really* messed up."

Hazarding a smile, she said, "At least you have a few years before he asks you to tell him about the day he was born. There's that."

"You always were the positive one in our circle," Toya commented.

"Was I too positive? Misery loves company, people say, so maybe now the circle will take me back." She'd meant to be sarcastic, but underneath was the question of why Toya and the others had retreated when they'd shared more than taste in fashion and preferences in wine. They'd shared ambitions and had been each other's cheerleaders.

"It's Las Vegas," Toya said decisively. "It's this town, and it's everyone trying to come out on top when there's only room for a few."

"No room for me, huh?" Shrugging, Bindi closed her purse and closed the door on a friendship that had never been there to begin with. "It was nice seeing you, Toya—"

"The coffee?" Toya shook her head as though to add, "Did you forget?"

"Sure, but when? This weekend ought to be fine."

"I'll call you. Where do you live?"

"In an apartment complex on East Dune."

"East Dune? Asher and his cronies call that street Strippers' Boulevard."

"I call it where I live. The ladies who live in my building are nice enough and keep to themselves, which I value more than having someone glued to my side when things are great but skip off in the other direction when things are hell." She headed for the restroom door. "Congratulations on your baby and your settlement."

She'd named them in order of importance, but likely Toya hadn't noticed.

"There's great news and not-so-great news," Bindi announced, her high heels sharp on the travertine tile in her apartment's modest-size kitchen. It reminded her of the one her childhood clubhouse had come equipped with. The clubhouse had been a flashy gift from her parents on her first Christmas after the overdose incident. To make up for so many restrictions that had come with being privately tutored and forever surrounded by adults whose conversation diets consisted of politics and business strategy, they'd had a construction company build her a minimansion, complete with travertine floors, tiny granite counters and crown molding. It'd been a magnificent gift, and she'd spent many lonely days and nights inside the house, until she'd outgrown it and her father had auctioned it off.

She hadn't cared all that much about the house anyway. It had always been the swing, something her father had designed during her mother's pregnancy and had constructed on the day Bindi was born. Toya's child would grow up and learn that his parents' marriage dissolution forms had spilled on the floor on the day he'd been born. At least Bindi could always treasure that her father had had the swing, with its cedar seat and vine-wrapped poly-twist rope, built for her.

Bindi smoothed the fringe hemline of her short red dress. After leaving Cleopatra's Barge, she'd changed her look, putting on a dress and makeup guaranteed to get her inside the La La Land club where she'd, fingers crossed, get the material she would need to earn sub-

stantial pay. "Great news? We're all going to survive
and thrive through the next several months if this gig
goes well. Not-so-great news? I'm staying overnight in
California."

Silence answered. Bindi gazed across the row of Chia
Pets and windowsill plants. A few had begun to lean during her week in the Seychelles, but they'd all survived
her neglect and now she was asking for their understand-
ing so she could jet out the door for an overnight jaunt to
Hollywood to pry into the supposed bad blood between
two hip-hop artists at a club notorious for having crime
scene tape up as often as its VIP ropes.

"I'm talking to plants," she said aloud, rubbing her
glossy red-painted lips together as she reached for the
pig. The pig was her favorite of the bunch. "I have a four-
hour I-15 drive ahead of me, and I'm standing in a my-
first-kitchen talking to plants."

Silently, she confided, *I'd rather stay home with you
than take this gig.*

Because if she said it aloud, she'd be forced to confront what it meant that she was so reluctant to find a
scoop and get paid for it. That was her job now. It was
behind-the-scenes and it allowed her luxuries: dinners
at casino restaurants, a kitchen stocked with gourmet
chocolate, memberships to landscaping and horticulture
clubs and engagement in eBay bidding wars for excellent finds, such as the Manolo Blahnik shoes decorating
her feet now.

Scandal sold, and she could either capitalize on it or
fail as a runt of a fish in a huge pond.

"Till tomorrow," she said, setting down the pig, turning out the kitchen pendant lights and going to the foyer
to collect her purse and overnight bag.

On the other side of the door came a pounding knock,

as if somebody had slammed a go-cart against it again and again. Tossing the bag and swinging up the bat, she went to the door and squinted through the peephole.

"Oh, my—"

"It's me!"

Toya Messa had been absent from Bindi's life for six months and was using the "It's me"? "Toya…what…" Fumbling with the row of locks, she shouted through the door, "Hang tight, okay?"

"This is a nicer building than I'd pictured," Toya commented conversationally, which meant on the other side of this door was a modelesque twentysomething wearing designer spring fashions and shouting in the hall. "How many locks do you *keep* on that door anyway?"

Bindi unlatched the final lock and opened the door. "I'm confused."

"We said we'd have coffee." Toya peeked around a squirming bundle. Fresh faced and bright eyed, she looked more like a teenager playing grown-up. Coach diaper bag, Christian Louboutin heels, Prada handbag, Tiffany cat's-eye glasses—

Bindi gave up trying to identify it all and simply opened the door wide. "Uh…come in." In her voice was inflection. It was better than outright asking, "Are you *sure* you meant to end up here?"

A squawk came from the bundle and Toya squeezed through, holding her baby in one arm and carrying a bassinet in the other hand. So *that* was what she'd used to knock on the door.

Bindi took the bassinet, glanced inside. Blankets and… "Are these walkie-talkies?"

"You're showing your age, thirtysomething."

"Not thirty*something*. I'm thirty."

"Miss Thirty, those are baby monitors." Toya muscled her stuff farther into the apartment, looking like the world's most fashionable vagrant. "Would you like to meet Holden?"

"Absolutely." Bindi had no siblings, so no nieces or nephews, and Toya was the only one in her group of wild gals who'd sealed her marriage with a child. Still, she could be captivated staring into the face of any baby. "Toya," she whispered, getting her first look at the chubby-cheeked brown-skinned baby, "you found it."

"What?" Toya sounded fatigued.

"Happiness."

"Oh," she scoffed. "Happiness weighs fifteen pounds and won't sleep."

Bindi giggled. "He's healthy, isn't he?"

"Healthy as a six-month-old baby."

"Then that's everything." Bindi cleared a basket of knitting supplies and a half-finished gingham-patterned blanket from the sofa. "Sit here. He smells like powder. Babies have the sweetest smells."

"It's always the women who don't have babies who say these things. It bewilders me. What comes out of this baby isn't sweet smelling at all." She unwrapped her son from his fleece blanket, threaded her fingers through his curly pale brown hair. "Mommy wants you to sleep."

Bindi knelt to set down the bassinet and remove the monitors. Why had she packed them for a nighttime cup of coffee? "Could he be teething?"

"He's not. He's stressed." As she spoke, baby Holden began to wail. "He must be picking it up from me. Babies can sense negative energy—did you know that?"

"I heard it before." Bindi thought it was a sad fact of life that children were exposed to the negativities of the world. No one was sheltering him from feeling his mother's stress, and who knew how Toya and her ex-husband interacted together in front of their son? "May I hold him?"

As they transferred the baby, his mother sighed and finally let the diaper bag and purse slip free of her clutches and she settled back against the sofa. "He keeps me on my toes. I've not only lost all of my baby weight, but I'm getting definition in my arms. Come bikini season, I'll be ready, jogging on the beach...pushing a stroller."

Bindi cuddled him against her chest, stroking his tiny back. His body quivered as his wailing began to subside. Turning to consult her clock, she started to worry about getting on the road in time to arrive at the club in Los Angeles before two o'clock, which was when her targets were expected to arrive. "Um, Toya—"

"He stopped crying." The woman's pitch dropped. "Is he asleep?"

He was, his Cupid's-bow mouth open, the dampness of tears on his eyelashes. He had his mother's eyelashes. Lucky kid. "Should I hand him back before he starts to drool on my dress?"

"Oh, your dress! I didn't notice you're all dressed to the nines. Were you on your way out?"

"Actually, yes."

"A date? Are you seeing someone, finally getting past Alessandro Franco?"

There were a few questions to tackle. Which should she answer first? If she honestly admitted she wasn't going on a date, but was driving out of town to chase down Hollywood drama, then she'd out herself as a tabloid rat. If she said she was seeing someone, Toya would harass her for details. And as far as her ex was concerned, she *was* over him in a romantic sense—which, she realized, had never existed. She wasn't over the hell he'd caused for her, so her decision to help his son find him would do more than bring him to justice's doorstep and give her material to turn over to *The Vegas Beat*. It would give her what she'd previously acknowledged as nothing but one of her mother's therapy vocabulary words: *closure.*

She'd meet closure, finality, and maybe then she could release the anger she kept bottled in her heart. She could seal it so tightly that even Toya's intuitive baby hadn't detected it. He'd found a peaceful and safe place in her arms, which stunned her because she was certain that she, with all her issues and her dirty past, could offer no one peace and safety.

"So is it a date?"

"It is. A date." Of sorts. What was a date anyway? An appointment? So infiltrating a shady Hollywood haunt to record some drama for the bloggers she had an allegiance to was, for all intents and purposes, a date.

Which said volumes about her romantic status.

"Let me guess. He's a CEO or an attorney or a—"

"No, Toya."

"Not a CEO or attorney?"

"I'd just rather not say."

Raising both eyebrows, the woman made a "hmm" noise. "I can respect that. But is he an older man? I see you finding a match with someone more like you—younger than Alessandro, but well-worn."

"I don't need dating advice." Who, after learning her past and the awful things she'd done, would want to date her? Who would love the broken pieces of her when she struggled to love them herself?

"Really listen, Bindi. You were fake happy with him. It's not worth it to marry someone like that. It's not worth it to be stuck in that way of life."

Bindi breathed in the baby's clean powder scent. "I don't dig anymore. I retired my shovel. I'm free."

"Yeah, you're free. Some girls can't get out."

"Here, take Holden." Bindi gently handed him back. "I'm going to get your coffee."

"Wait. Can I ask a favor?"

"What is it?"

Toya looked down at her baby, but when she lifted her face, it was streaked with tears and her mouth was starting to curl. This was the onset of an ugly cry. "Would you let Holden and me stay here for a while?"

*What?*

"Why? Your divorce settlement—"

"Asher's having it voided. Be-because of the baby!"

Holden sputtered in his sleep, and Bindi cradled him so Toya could be free to grapple for a pillow and shove her face into its plushness. "I'm sorry I married him. After the baby was born, he—he said he'd had a vasectomy and Holden couldn't be his biological son. And I—" Toya dumped the pillow onto the floor, swallowed and rubbed her already puffy face. "I believed him. I fell for the trap."

"I'm not following, Toya."

"I had to admit that I was with somebody else, because I panicked that the other man could've been…" She gripped Bindi's shoulder. "It was a lie. Asher never had a vasectomy, and Holden *is* his baby. But when I admitted someone else could've been the father, his lawyers came down on me because when we got married, I agreed to a fidelity clause. It was a mistake."

"Cheating on Asher?"

"Marrying him. He gave me a choice—give up my parental rights to Holden or give up the settlement. He says that since I violated the clause, technically he has grounds to take back the settlement and give me hell in court. And tonight I made my decision, so here I am, a single mom."

"What made you decide tonight?"

"Inspiration. You, Bindi. I wasn't there for you when Alessandro turned, and we stopped being friends for no good reason. But you fought all by yourself. You got out and you're living here and making a life for yourself. I can be like you, can't I?"

"Be like me?" For so long she'd been an antonym of the term *role model*. She never would've believed that a sparkling young woman like Toya Messa would hit incredible heights in society, then wind up looking to her for guidance. "My universe isn't perfect."

"I know, but it's real. Will you let Holden and I stay here for a while, please? He likes you and he doesn't cry all the time. And I can…hmm…I can help clean up around the apartment." Toya looked right, then she looked left, then— "Is that a pole?"

Bindi eyed the pole, which she'd strung twinkling lights around to pseudodisguise its purpose. "It is. This apartment's a sublet. It belongs to a showgirl."

*"Oh."* She pointed to the ornamented balsam-fir tree near the kitchen and the menorah on the faux fireplace's mantel. "Which do you celebrate?"

"Both. Neither. It's complicated."

"Okay. But it *is* February. It's time to pack it all away. Oh, and I can help with that!"

"Deal," Bindi said, because she was put on the spot and because she saw too much of herself in Toya Messa. She turned on the TV, handed the remote to the young woman. "Roomies?"

"Roomies. And friends. Real friends this time."

Bindi settled back against the sofa, hugged the baby

close even though she immediately warned herself to not become too attached. In a minute she'd contact the bloggers and pass up the opportunity to spy on A-list celebrities in favor of a night at home with a friend and a baby who deserved all the peace and safety Bindi could offer.

"What about your date?" Toya asked.

"No." Bindi signaled for her to click the listing for a reality TV show centered on brides-to-be deciding on wedding dresses, and Toya snorted at the irony because it'd be a while before either saw themselves in a white gown. "I just decided that I don't want to be so focused on life that I forget to live."

# Chapter 7

As the doors to the glass elevator at the east wing of Constant and Spencer and Associates' Law Offices parted mutely and a seductively robotic female voice overhead announced, "Floor three," Santino knew he wouldn't like the reason his father's attorneys had summoned him here.

Shortly after his brief exchange with Attorney Chuck Constant, his brother had sent him a text message and they'd deduced that the spur-of-the-moment meeting was suspicious and they'd both be there.

Exiting the elevator, he entered a lobby spacious enough to host a parade and resembled an exclusive club more than a legal firm. It made sense—the attorneys only represented high-profile clients and could afford to treat them accordingly. A six-foot water feature depicted streams flowing from Lady Justice's scales. The polished black floor reflected the parallel rows of recessed lights that parted ways to form halos over twin reception desks. Chuck Constant had been the one to personally contact Santino, so he went to the desk that had *Constant* engraved into the facade. As he'd had to do to gain entry past main-floor security, he authenticated his identify on a touch-screen computer. Instead of being directed past metal detectors, he was now immediately offered baked goods from a basket and a drink of his pleasure from a double-tier cart.

"Might I recommend a daiquiri?" the woman steering the cart inquired, coming to a clean stop in front of him. She, along with the other receptionists in the lobby—a symmetrical three per desk—wore all formfitting black, except she stood out with the bite of a pink hairpin in her raked-back curls.

Magdalene Kist, her name tag declared.

*Aw, hell.*

They'd met before, when she'd accompanied Chuck Constant and Waylon Spencer to a dinner meeting to meet with Santino and his father. That'd been months ago, when Santino believed the Las Vegas Slayers had been forced from his father's hands and he'd wanted to conquer heaven and hell to see it returned to Franco ownership. Actually, he and Magdalene had done more than "met."

She'd murmured the sexiest "Pleasure to meet you" he'd ever heard when she'd enclosed his hand in both of hers for a shake. He'd liked that. Her ass had swayed in a zebra-print skirt when she'd hurried up from the table to fix his coffee on one of her boss's directives. He'd *really* liked that. And in the guest services corridor, when him heading to the men's room and her leaving the ladies' room, she'd cut into his path and kissed him—and he'd let it happen. Only when her hand had slid from his chest down toward his crotch did he interrupt her, because her effect on him had been too weak and he'd known without going through the motions of trying to force arousal that ultimately they'd both be left unsatisfied.

Magdalene would've joined the parade of women who'd fantasized, tried to gratify, ached to be touched or were hungry for commitment, only to wind up pissed off when he didn't measure up to expectation. So he'd rejected her as considerately as he could, but she still had sulked through the rest of the business dinner, hanging on to a daiquiri.

"No, thanks, Magdalene," he said, declining the drink and any ideas she might be entertaining about a do-over of their last encounter. "A bottle of water's fine."

She removed the cap from a bottle and presented it with a smile as she gave his suit a once-over. "I'm working closely with Attorney Constant today. Your brother, Nate, hasn't arrived yet. If you'll follow me, I'll escort you to the conference room upstairs."

Santino walked with her to a flight of stairs, and as they ascended, she said, "Santino, I feel I should warn you."

He stopped, looked over his shoulder. "About?"

"The group is stepping back from your father's case. That's why Attorney Constant called you and your brother. Where things stand now, the Henderson property and the majority of his remaining assets will be forfeited if they're connected to the game fixing. The Nevada Gaming Commission has produced enough evidence of unregulated gambling activity that your godfather has been trying to pass off as his casino's profits to disprove him. The casino's licensed and the side sports wagering, of course, wasn't legally handled." Magdalene's expression turned earnest. "The NFL's conducting an independent investigation of all his moves as owner, but there are enough former players and staff coming forward, very quietly, to make the initial charges stick. One of those players is Jimar Fray."

Jimar Fray was the former defensive Slayer whose cash-bought illegal tackle had sent Santino into surgery. After a personal-foul penalty and an expertly prepared public statement apologizing for conduct that injured an opponent, he'd slipped out of the league and hadn't found a job with another team. After rehabbing himself, Santino hadn't come for Jimar. He'd on some level accepted the incident as gameplay and had wanted to move on—until his father had admitted to paying Jimar to stop number 85's block and rush assaults on the field by any means necessary. Jimar continued to lay low, and Santino was waiting him out.

But now… "He's out of hiding?"

"He's talking now."

"Constant and Spencer want to wash their hands, huh?"

"With no one to defend, they have to cut their losses. Your godfather's casino's on the block, too, since it head-quartered the gambling ring. *Allegedly.* Just waiting for convictions. And, uh, it doesn't exactly help that Alessandro split while the feds and the NFL have him under investigation. Pretty sure he's looking at federal custody and losing all his toys." She smoothed her hand over his sleeve. "I'm telling you this so you aren't blindsided."

"Why are you telling me this, and not my brother?"

"You were the man at that business dinner sitting at his father's side and ready to fight for him. Your brother wasn't."

No, because Nate was smart. A former Slayers athletic trainer, he'd come to a point where trying to reclaim the Slayers hadn't seemed worth it, and now he was gunning for a PhD and had his former rival, Charlotte Blue, cheering him on at every checkpoint.

The damn kid had had it right all along. Yeah, that made him smart.

"Why else are you debriefing me?" Santino asked Magdalene when her hand remained on his sleeve.

"I..." The hand fell away. "I took a huge risk, telling you all this, putting myself out there like that."

"Why?"

"Because of a stupid crush. Because I thought I might have a good-looking football player to myself for a little while. Because the attorneys are dropping Alessandro and I thought that if I didn't act fast, I'd lose the nerve to show you that I like you."

*And she wanted you to like her, dumb ass.* On a shallow level, he did. But below the surface was emptiness.

"I'm not here because I want to be liked," he said, continuing up the stairs. "I'm here for business. And you wouldn't want me, Magdalene."

"How do you know without giving me a chance? One kiss isn't enough to show you the possibilities."

"It is, though. One kiss is enough." One impulsive kiss that shouldn't have happened but was inevitable, like a tragedy destined to screw up what had once made sense, had been all he'd needed on Cora Island with Bindi. One touch of her mouth had convinced him that he'd needed more and had urged him on until he'd gotten to the point where he couldn't quit replaying it as though he were reviewing films and trying to discern where he'd botched a game-winning reception. "Another kiss isn't going to happen for us."

"What changed?" she asked.

Bindi had changed. But so had he. And they were meeting in the middle, figuring themselves out as they figured out each other. How friggin' problematic was that? "I can't hold up more than a professional relationship with you. And hey, going back to what you told me, after this meeting, we won't have even that. If a football player's who you're after, this city's got a team full of them. Take a page from the men who sign your paycheck and cut your losses."

Magdalene clicked her teeth together. "Humph. Message clear, then. Are you going to request a different assistant? I'm sure Attorneys Constant and Spencer will be accommodating, but I hope you'll reconsider reporting my…conduct."

"No. Let's finish this."

Together they strode into a glass-walled center office finished in black, silver and white. Assembled were Chuck Constant and Waylon Spencer. The men had enough respect to spare him the toothy grins and claps on the back before gesturing to a leather seat across from them. At the head of the table Magdalene sat before a stack of files and a tablet.

When Nate entered, frowning in a way that reminded Santino of himself, Magdalene closed the door, resumed her seat and said nothing, as her bosses launched into their resignation announcement. The men weren't in a sharing mood. They pressured him for information he didn't have, complained about paddling knee-deep into Alessandro's case only to be screwed over and ultimately announced that when—or if—he returned to Nevada, he'd need to find himself new representation.

Alessandro's case was a sinking ship, and now that his lawyers had figured out that abandoning it was their only route to a lifeboat, the people who were left behind to drown were Santino and his brother.

"We didn't invite you here just to say, 'We're done, get out,'" said Chuck, motioning for his assistant to fork over a file. "Santino, Nate, the management of Futuro needs to be addressed."

Santino glanced across the table at the assistant, but she continued to sit silently, feigning extreme interest in her files as she had with a daiquiri months ago. "Management of Futuro? Isn't that tied into Dad's—"

"Got to stop you there," the attorney said. "There are a few technicalities you boys aren't aware of. Gloria Franco took ownership of Alessandro's eyewear company decades ago. He'd apparently given it to her as a gift, and for whatever reason they continued to let you believe he was managing it. She took a few precautions, setting up trusts and savings bonds, that sort of thing, all right? But look, it was arranged for an independent entity to ghost manage the company in the event of her death. Should Alessandro die, become physically or mentally incapacitated—you get the point—the responsibility to maintain Futuro as a privately held company, take it public or dissolve it entirely would fall on the two of you equally. It's protection."

"Our father's MIA," Nate said. "Santino and I don't believe he's right in the head, but who can confirm whether he's incapacitated at all if he can't be found?"

The attorney flipped pages, frowned down at the paperwork. "After a twelve-month waiting period, ownership would transfer. If you want to speed up the process, you'll find out where he's hiding. If you want to go for insanity—I'll say it one more time—you'll find out—"

"We get it," Santino said. But he wasn't concerned with hanging on to a family-owned company. If Al had ever seen in himself the mental slippage that others could see, then he'd had to consider the insanity route. What did he have to gain by vanishing and leaving behind all of his possessions?

Again, the thought occurred that Gian DiGorgio was involved.

Outside the conference room, Santino and his brother walked in silence. Nate wore his anger quietly, but the gritty despair screamed in the restless clenching of his fists and the jumping lightning streak of a vein above one eyebrow. "I didn't look after Dad. She asked me to."

"Mom?"

"Yeah. She asked me to do that, then we lost her, then I took some steps back. I didn't walk into his warfare. You did that, moving back into the house."

"A houseful of staff made stuff convenient when I was trying to get back on my feet," Santino said.

"Nah, you can hang on to the 'good son' badge, Santino. He loved you for taking care of the family. He was proud of you."

"His love and his pride put me on a surgeon's table, man. I don't want to hear all that. I want to find him. I'm in limbo, on hold like Futuro. I have to face him."

"What if you can't face him?" Nate stopped him in the hall, his voice low. "We never said this, but it's been three weeks now and I can't sleep through a damn night anymore because I'm thinking that this is more than just a man on the run. I got my woman sitting up at night with me, trying to convince me that I can't start grieving that man until I know he's really gone."

A week had passed since he'd traveled to the Seychelles. Bindi had nothing to report. Neither had Zaf nor Cecelia Whit. But that didn't mean his father was dead. People said dead men tell no tales. They hadn't met Alessandro Franco. In the flesh he wreaked trouble. Beyond the grave he'd be merciless.

"Go home," Santino said to his brother. "Go home and kiss your woman and tell her she's right. You can't grieve him yet."

Nate hesitated, shooting a hand through his short hair. "Don't say you're in limbo. Dad said that right after Mom died, and you know what he did."

"Married, divorced, married, divorced."

"Yeah. Don't do that. Don't get married without warning me first." He looked him in the eye then. "'Cause I'm giving you that respect now. Charlotte. I'm going to marry her."

Santino could've asked if Nate knew was certain he could trust her, could've advised him to hold off on account of what he'd been told about her DEA friend's involvement in forcing open the Pandora's box that had held all kinds of diseased secrets. Instead he said, "She sits up with you at night when you're stressing. Damn straight, you're going to marry her."

"I'm moving on. You compared yourself to Futuro—take it. You and I don't need the money, but your life's in intermission, man, and it's time to change that."

Santino had grown his NFL income and hadn't been as roughed up with bad business endeavors as many former players. His finance analyst suggested he capitalize on the circumstances of his retirement and open a physical therapy center. His sports agent kept coming to him with commentator offers, but the man now knew Santino wanted to be back on the field. He wanted his feet back on the turf, and not even his brother knew his undertakings and that an NFL comeback might be the only sense of rightness that would let him sleep through the night.

No, he wouldn't be moving on from professional football, but he'd be moving forward with his life.

"I got to go," he said to Nate. "I know a woman who needs to move on."

The bushes were different. That was the only physical change Santino detected about the Franco family mansion when he parked his truck in the wide driveway. They'd been cut down to circles and slim cylinder shapes, and no longer had the uniqueness or personality they'd had when a certain woman had lived here.

All while Bindi was trying to sculpt the house to become her home, he'd battled her. He'd resisted her influence, refused to see past the surface, concerned himself with the fact that she hadn't been the right woman for his father. He should've been sharp enough to realize that his father hadn't been the right man for her.

Though he kept his entry keys, Santino entered the house as though he were a guest. It wasn't his home. Nadia, who greeted him graciously at the door, with her uniform pressed and spotless as though she still had an employer to answer to, wasn't his housekeeper. But he'd come here to change that.

"What can I do for you?" Nadia asked, allowing him to drift from one room to the next.

He almost stepped into the room that held the baby grand piano, almost walked right in and started playing. He almost forgot, just that suddenly, that this place wasn't his home and the piano wasn't his to touch. "You can come work for me," he said to her, facing her in time to see the crease of wrinkles deepen on her forehead. "I have a condo that's half the size of this house and only half as clean. You can save me, Nadia."

She smiled. "Santino, I'm not leaving until I'm forced out. The house still belongs to your father."

"It won't for long. I want to see you taken care of."

"It's about loyalty."

"God, Nadia, the era's ended. Dad's not your boss anymore."

The housekeeper settled her hands on his cheeks, patted the bristly stubble with the heels of her hands. "You have this beard, but you're looking like him now. You and Alessandro wear *tiredness* the same." She sighed.

"My, but both so handsome. My loyalty isn't to him. It's to Gloria."

"Mom wouldn't have asked you to stay here forever."

"Of course not. She was my friend, and smart as a whip."

*Smart as a whip.* "Did she tell you about Futuro?"

"There were two heads of household when she was alive. She stood beside your father, not behind him." Nadia finally nodded her confirmation. "I knew she controlled the company and wanted a soft place for you and Nate to land, if it came to that. But I don't think it was because she didn't trust her husband."

"He gambled—hell, he taught Nate and me cards and had Gian schooling us in table games. If he was hooked all along, he curbed it for Mom."

"Suppose he turned to it after she died. That's what my heart says, and I feel sorry for him. Grief took too much from that man."

"Are you still here because of sympathy?"

"No, I told you—for Gloria. She asked me to help her maintain a home for her family. I'm still doing that. You left before, Santino, and didn't come back to stay until after the injury. But you did come back."

"The house is wrapped up in Dad's mess, Nadia. You will have to leave."

"Until then, I'm staying. Let me do this for Gloria. I want to know that I made every effort to keep my word to that lady. Okay, Santino?"

"All right."

She lightly slapped his cheeks, smiling kindly, then turned for the kitchen. "Now get in here and eat something. You're all muscle-bound now, but you're not eating enough. Or sleeping well. I can tell, you know. I've a good mind to feed you turkey so you can rest."

"Is that the tryptophan thing you're talking about? Yeah, that doesn't work on me. I can eat turkey, if you got it, but I'm still going to be wide-awake and bothering the hell out of you until you get out of this place."

Nadia sighed. "I don't have turkey, smart-ass. That was a bluff."

"So I called your bluff and you've got nothing to back it up?" He tsked. "Tell you what. I'll settle for that box you and the others packed up for Bindi Paxton. You still have it?"

"That woman?" Nadia made a rude noise, pretended to spit. "Ah, I understand. The house *has* been feeling off since Alessandro brought her here, and now I know why it still does. Yes, her things are in a box off the main hall."

"Hey, Nadia."

"Yes?"

"We can't blame her for what went wrong. I thought I could, but I was wrong as hell for it."

Without comment, the housekeeper left the kitchen then came back shortly afterward with a packing box that contained a layer of…stuff. It wasn't clothes or jewelry, but a scatter of items from a miniflashlight to a palm tree key chain. Pawing through, discovering a tiny wooden tic-tac-toe game, he thought about how Bindi had looked standing on Villa Soleil's veranda with candlelight touching her and that incredible "should I smile or shouldn't I?" smirk.

Prying into her privacy and taking the fast track to learn about her past, Santino had cheated himself out getting to know her. He deserved that sense of loss. She was more than a means to an end, and damn, did he want to see her now.

Santino's phone vibrated, and he pulled it from his pocket.

Speaking of Bindi Paxton, according to her text message, she needed a favor.

Twenty-four hours hadn't passed yet, but Bindi considered her friend Toya missing. The evening before Toya had swept out of the apartment, kissing her son on the head and thanking Bindi for agreeing to babysit while she took care of something.

Bindi hadn't pressed her for particulars. "Something" was what they said to be vague, to say, "It's none of your business and I don't feel like sharing." She'd gone out for somethings twice over the past week, gathering camera-phone photos to send to the bloggers, who'd forgiven her Los Angeles fail and had offered her the opportunity to redeem herself with fresh material.

Last night after she'd forgone a yoga workout to feed Toya's son and rock him to sleep, she'd put the boy in the crib his mother had bought the day after they'd moved in. Then she'd gone to bed with a baby monitor beside her where a man should be. When sunshine and Holden's angry wails had awakened her early this morning, she'd stumbled from her bedroom to find the sofa vacant and no sign of Toya.

With no car seat, Bindi had been grounded the entire day. Feedings and diaper changing and pep talks to a child who might not understand her words but would sense her worry had interrupted her pacing and redialing of Toya's cell phone number.

She hadn't wanted to drag authorities into the situation prematurely or reach out to Asher Messa. If Toya was fine and police caught a scent of child abandonment, her ex-husband would only have more ammo to annihilate her in their already nasty divorce.

So she'd made a decision that she hoped wouldn't end up a ginormous mistake.

Bindi peeked over the edge of the crib, where Holden rested peacefully. He should be peaceful now—fifteen minutes ago he'd regurgitated on her shirt. Since the first thing she'd grabbed to throw on was a designer high-low top, she hoped his tummy was settled. For the seventh or eighth time since she'd texted Santino, she looked at their conversation on the screen.

I need a favor.

In under a minute he'd responded. Name it.

A car seat. Something that'll fit a 6 mo. old.

Then, Okay.

Santino hadn't asked for her address, and she'd figured he wouldn't have to, because if he knew the color of her luggage then he probably knew where she was staying, as well.

Refusing to start pacing again, Bindi sat on the sofa but sprang up again at the grating sound of the buzzer.

"I've got that favor you asked for," Santino said through the intercom, and Bindi sagged against the wall.

*He came through for me.*

They weren't friends, were bound by an alliance to find his father and were absolute trouble together, but he'd come through for her.

Bindi opened the door at his knock, and caught her breath at the sight of him standing in the hall wearing a suit and holding a new-in-box infant car seat. When he set the box down just inside the door, she was so damn glad. Because his arms were free now to hold her.

She knew he would.

She knew, as she lurched forward and kissed him, that he'd stand right there and hold her.

"Are we going to talk about that kiss?"

Stretched across the rear passenger bench in her Jeep Grand Cherokee and adjusting Holden Messa's cap while Santino leaned in from the opposite side to secure the rear-facing car seat's harness, Bindi thought it'd be easier to avoid his question if he weren't close enough to maul again. "Your hands are in my way," she said when their fingers brushed and she quickly reached to straighten the soft cap on the baby's head. He was snug and safe in the cushioned seat and watching her so calmly that she felt a little bit elated and a whole lot nervous that he trusted his young life to her.

She had no reason to linger in this position, but she was gravitating toward the comfort that she had no business finding in either of these males. It was too easy to form an attachment to a baby, but what was her excuse for the weird, undefined bond materializing between her and a man who'd brought a car seat to her door? "They're huge. You could palm basketballs with those."

"Yeah, actually, you're right," Santino said, and when she shot a glance at him, he was watching her steadily. "I can put them someplace else, if that's what you want." With a click, he fastened the five-point harness's buckle and settled that hand on her shoulder. "Is that what you want? Me to touch you here?"

The touch was a hybrid of gentle and bold—just enough to give her a whiff of sensual possibilities and a hint of promise. Instantly lulled, she let her eyes start to drift, then felt his fingers move to her lips. She kissed one knuckle, then the next, then added the lightest of bites to the inside of his wrist before she got herself together. "Stop it."

Withdrawing, he said, "If we're not going to talk about that kiss in your apartment, I've got some more questions. For instance, whose baby is this?"

*You mean all your sophisticated tracking couldn't clue you in that Toya Messa and her infant are my new roommates?*

In the apartment, when she'd finally stepped back from their kiss and immediately started buzzing around to collect her friend's son and the diaper bag and the checklist she'd printed from the Shopping for Baby page of SoYoureaMommy.com, she'd assumed he wouldn't make an issue of her action. It was more of a reflex anyway. It wasn't as though she'd drummed her fingers together and meditated jumping him at the door.

When he hadn't demanded any explanation, just cradled the baby so expertly that she'd been ashamed to silently worry that he might hold the infant as he had held a football, she'd thought he wasn't interested in the details of any mishaps she'd found her way into.

But he'd only been biding his time.

"What I know for certain is that you weren't pregnant when you lived in Henderson. Surrogate? Adoption?"

"He's not mine," she said, easing out of the car to shut the door.

Late in the afternoon, the parking lot of her building was at its busiest, as most of the tenants worked night shifts. Some women toted out garment bags and makeup cases; others urged young backpack-carrying kids to hurry along and watch for traffic.

Her phone dinged, signaling a text message. She clutched her phone. *Toya!*

I'm okay.

Bindi quickly punched a response. Where are you?

A reply came quickly. Somewhere.

That wasn't going to wash. *Somewhere* didn't apply for a woman not coming home to her child.

Bindi repeated her previous question, but the phone didn't ding.

"Get in," she said to Santino when he shut his door. "If you want answers, you'll have to come along for the ride. The truck will be fine and we won't be gone long."

"Where are we going?"

"Somewhere very, very ordinary. Although to a high roller it might seem foreign. We're off to Target. The baby needs things."

"I've been to Target," he said, settling in the passenger's seat beside her. "Tabitha had a personal shopper hook her up with everything from shoes to soap, but I figured it was less of a hassle to get my own stuff. When I want a bag of chips, I get a bag of chips. It never made sense to draft a proxy."

"And you braved a mob of football fans every time?"

"Sometimes. It's part of sports and entertainment though."

Bindi activated the child-lock system, turned the key, glanced through the rearview mirror at another woman's precious baby and suddenly felt different. Motherly? Responsible? She couldn't pin it. "Well, Santino, the baby who drooled on your suit is Holden Messa. His father owns Messa Technologies, and last week his mom popped up in front of my apartment looking for a place to stay.

So while Toya and her ex-husband get their problems worked out, she and I are bringing up baby. She's been gone for a while and I want to track her down, but the baby's running low on some things."

"Toya. She was one of the girls you ran with last year. Kind of surprising."

"What?"

"That she'd get married without insurance."

Bindi tried to block the sting of offense, but it got to her anyway. The truth had venom. She and the others had been all about self-protection, warding off prenups and searching for almost fatherly security in marriages to rich, powerful, older men. "She thought she had insurance, but there was a loophole that revealed her hubby to be a horrible father and—" Bristling, she took a breath and a right at the intersection. "Listen, they both made awful decisions and now their only child is so stuck in the middle that he's counting on me and he doesn't even know how scary that is."

Santino cast a look toward the backseat, though the baby faced the rear of the vehicle. "He seems to be okay with you."

"And you. Thanks for not holding him like a football. I thought you would and I was prepared to grab him."

The man's laughter made her feel as gooey as an oven-warmed chocolate-chip cookie. "I've got distant cousins and friends who think procreating is a nice hobby. Might not be long before I have a nephew. Or a niece."

Bindi's eyes bugged and her tabloid fodder sensors glared. The bloggers loved baby-bump stories almost as much as sex scandals. "Is Charlotte Blue pregnant?"

"No, but Nate's marrying her. He told me today."

"Why did you tell me?" she asked. She was damn

skilled at hiding her freelance activities, but he couldn't deny he didn't fully trust her.

"I want to see what you'll do with the information."

"I won't tell anyone," she said, and was taken aback by her own decision. "Charlotte and Nate aren't people I want to hurt, so it wouldn't be worth it, now, would it?"

Santino was silent for a beat. "Okay. Point is, I know how to handle a baby."

"Oh, then it makes total sense why you didn't freak when Holden gurgled spit bubbles on your Armani jacket."

"It's not the end of the world. It's just the beginning of his." Santino touched her thigh. It was more an encouraging gesture than anything sexual. "You're doing all right with the kid."

"For a woman who's not fit to care for plants?" She meant to sound playful, but it came out a lot more anxious than intended.

"You're okay, Bindi."

At the store, they opted for efficiency, ripped the shopping list in half and took separate carts. Bindi was in the laundry-care aisle, debating between two brands of safe-for-baby detergent with Holden preoccupied with slobbering on his plump fingers, when Santino's cart parked beside hers.

"You're going to block the aisle," she warned, going all gooey chocolate again. The guy had on an expensive suit and was confidently pushing around a cart half-filled with diapers, wipes and bottles. His hands were large, dexterous and multitalented. She wouldn't mind having them on her again. "Did you find everything?"

"Yeah. Check the list." He gave her the list and she compared it to the contents in the cart.

"Well done." She lifted a fist for a bump. "Boom."

"What about you?"

"Almost," she said, choosing a jug of detergent to put at the bottom of the cart. Cooing to the baby, "Bindi needs something now." She nudged her cart forward and reached for a box of dryer sheets.

"That—" Santino took the box, sniffed it and looked her up and down. His mouth inched up at the corner. "You smell like dryer sheets."

"I like to put them in my dresser and closet."

Santino edged closer so he could whisper in her ear, "That's so damn hot. I don't know why, but it is."

"So add it to the list of things you like about me."

"Why'd you kiss me at your apartment?"

"Can't let that go, can you?"

"Uh-uh. We can talk about the stripper pole another time."

"I kissed you because I wanted to. Reason enough?"

*You're cute—flirting with a man who had you tailed to the Seychelles. Get over it. Remember to get over it.*

Except she wasn't getting over it, and she suddenly felt trapped again. Despite all of her new goals, all the effort to reinvent herself, she was still getting ensnared in the sort of drama she'd meant to leave behind.

"I got things from here," she said, clearing her throat to get rid of the panic she could taste there. "I can drive you back for your truck."

"I'll take care of it. Not a problem. But what's up with you?"

"We—we're tripping if we can act as if this is normal. Shopping together like a daddy and mommy with a baby. The baby isn't mine and you're not mine and I can't get attached to either of you." Wigging out in a market wasn't the most pleasant way to *get over it*, but it gave her the oomph to transfer the items from his cart to hers and start making her way toward the checkout lanes. "I'll pay you back for the car seat," she called over her shoulder.

"With dinner."

*Uh...huh?* "What?"

"Dinner. Food. Good food, hopefully. I'm asking you out to dinner."

Bindi looked at the baby, but he only stared back at her curiously. "B-but I can't commit to that. The baby."

"Another day, then."

"If she doesn't say yes, I'll go," a woman volunteered eagerly, and Bindi finally noticed the smattering of shoppers who'd paused to get all up in her business.

"She's going to say yes," Santino said.

Narrowing her eyes, because she didn't want to imagine him having dinner with that woman or any other, unreasonable as it was, she shouted, "Yes, okay?"

People laughed and murmured and stared, and when the shopper said to him, "Hmm, well, can I get an autograph?" Bindi left him occupied with his superstar life and she returned to her ordinary one.

# Chapter 8

*Paris.*

Bindi studied her smartphone, examining the one-word response from Toya. She turned it sideways, then upside down, then tossed the device into her Grand Cherokee's cup holder.

Darkness was starting to hover over the palm trees lining the streets. The baby was fussy—no doubt bored to be spending so much time in a car seat, no matter how state of the art it was. Bindi had forgotten to rescue her impulse-buy chocolate bar from the cheery red-and-white shopping bags she'd loaded into the back of her vehicle.

*Now* she was pissed.

Paris? As in France? Not likely, even if Toya had gotten control of the Messa company jet. So as in *on her way* to Paris? No. That didn't sound right. She'd seen the love on Toya's face when she'd bathed her son in the sink and when she'd stood so still next to the crib, watching him sleep. She wouldn't skip the country and leave behind the child she loved.

Except, it wasn't unheard of. Child abandonment happened for a multitude of reasons. People left the ones they loved all the time. This very second, someone was giving up a future with someone they cared about.

Bindi swallowed—she was thirsty and her palms were

getting uncomfortably clammy on the steering wheel. "Paris? *Le Paris*."

Then, as though a rolling shade been snapped open to reveal the clarity of a bright, open window, it made sense. Paris Las Vegas.

"Hang on, honey," she said aloud, redirecting her course. "We're going to find Mommy."

When Bindi at last confronted the glorious hotel casino, with its Eiffel Tower roof and nothing but temptation in the air, she gingerly switched the car seat's handle from one hand to the other. Carrying a fifteen-pound infant bundled inside a heavy-duty carrier was all the workout her arms needed today.

Where to begin in this place, she wondered, considering all the places Toya could be. The woman attended London Fashion Week last year, had no shame in modeling trends and advertising top designers' handiwork, so she wouldn't be hiding out in Paris Las Vegas. So she'd be visible, with attention on her.

Bindi only hoped Toya wasn't gambling—she wouldn't attempt to venture into a gambling room with the baby.

She considered the restaurants, scrolling through her mental Rolodex for memories of her experiences dining in these places. She'd lived in Las Vegas for years, and it seemed every moment had been filled with seeking all the luxury the city had to offer a twentysomething living off the endless supply of wealthy men's money.

She chose Gordon Ramsay Steak because the restaurant was said to be upscale and, if she was recalling her old circle's outing to a famous restaurant in Los Angeles, where the chef had come to their table and requested that he personally prepare their menu, Toya could really put away a steak.

Inside the restaurant, the high technology and glimmering luxury had her mouth watering. Or it was the delicious aromas of everything she wouldn't mind sitting down and sampling?

Focusing on locating her friend, she feigned ignorance when people casually glanced up from their digital menus to frown at her and leaned forward in their high-backed chairs to murmur to each other as she shuffled past with the carrier's handle in both hands.

Bindi's hair had by now slipped free of the bobby pins she'd stuck all over her head this morning, her top was wrinkled and she had a burp cloth draped over one shoulder.

*Give it up*, she considered snapping to the downstairs dining room at large. *Have you never had a hot-mess day?*

She'd almost given up when she noticed a mane of curly dark hair on the dining room's second story. Taking the stairs cautiously, she carted little Holden. "Where have you been, Toya?"

Toya, in a white one-shouldered wrap dress, sat alone at a table with a single goblet of wine in front of her… and a scatter of balled-up tissues. She looked up at Bindi through tear-filled eyes. "I'm sorry!"

"Shh. Silent ugly cry is okay," she said, setting down the car seat and taking the seat next to her friend, "but start bawling and you might get us ushered out."

Toya scooted her chair and dropped against her shoulder, hiccupping.

"Wait a second," Bindi said, dislodging herself to flip over the burp cloth. "There. Cry."

Waitstaff attentively gravitated to their table, but Bindi politely fielded their inquiries and offers for assistance. One woman all gussied up with runny mascara and in the throes of a bawl-fest and the other wilted and wrinkled accessorizing with a burp cloth and a transportable car seat could draw a crowd.

But starting the second act of your life, whether you were a twenty-five-year-old divorced single mom or a thirty-year-old secret tabloid rat with a sketchy past and an unfortunate connection to a white-collar criminal, wasn't guaranteed to be pretty or painless.

Sometimes you had to cry the tears and swim across to get to the other side.

"I can't help you if you try to figure this out on your own," Bindi said gently. "Have you been here at Paris since last night?"

"No. First I went home—to his house."

"Asher's?"

"Yes. He texted me yesterday, asked me to meet up with him. It was this big freaking ambush. His legal team was there, at the house, and they surrounded me and he asked me to change my name. He said Holden can keep his last name, since the paternity test he'd had ordered confirmed the biological match. But he wants me to give up Messa and go back to Keech."

"Toya…" Bindi awkwardly patted her curly hair. She'd never been the there-there type—she had learned by her mother's example that compassion wasn't necessarily innate, but she had to do something that might be comforting. "Listen, Toya Messa is a woman bound to a man who doesn't want her. Toya Keech is a woman ready to get cracking on her second chance. You don't need his name. You belong to you."

"I took a bunch of my clothes," Toya said, sitting up and leaving the mascara-smeared cloth on Bindi's shoulder, "and stuffed them in my car. I put on this dress and I've been at this hotel for hours, wondering if… I wanted to see if anyone… God, I'm pathetic."

"You wondered if a man like Asher Messa would come along?" Bindi understood. She'd been in this position before—but she hadn't allowed her broken engagement to send her back into the cycle. "Starting over hurts. I know it. But it gets better, Toya. Someone who's good for you comes into your life." For Bindi, it was a man she hadn't let herself anticipate. Beneath all the complicated threads, Santino Franco was undefined and new and sexy and dangerous—as hopeful as it was risky. Chances were it would be over the second he tracked down his father and found out she'd one-upped him, but until then, she'd enjoy the kissing. The sex. Being asked out to dinner on a real, honest-to-God date. When was the last time *that* had happened?

"Your baby is right here." Bindi removed the burp cloth and scooped the infant from the car seat to pass to his mother. "Did you drink this wine or have any other drinks? I'm going to call a car service so you won't drive home emotional and intoxicated."

"I didn't drink and the tears are gone. I'm fine to drive back to East Dune."

"Please don't look past him or let fear come between you. Just take him home and hug him."

"Okay. What are you going to do?"

"Don't know. Maybe I'll buy myself a steak." She watched Toya stand up with the baby tucked tight against her. "I won't hang out here too long. There are baby goods in my Jeep."

"You didn't have a car seat. Where did this come from?"

"A friend brought it over so Holden and I could hit the road."

"One of the girls?"

"No," she said with a wistful smile. The circle was

broken and the girls had kept their distance. "A different friend."

"A man? Who?"

"Someone," she said elusively. It was a much neater answer than "My ex-fiancé's son, the man I had unforgettable Valentine's sex with on the Seychelles. The man who's possibly still having me tailed and, yes, the guy I agreed to sell out for some steady employment."

That last part gave her bats in the stomach. It wasn't that she owed Santino her loyalty—she owed him nothing at all. But she felt guilty all the same, as though she was hanging on too tightly to tactics that had never benefitted her.

"We should set up a system, should you and Mister Someone want a sleepover at the apartment. Bra on the doorknob?"

"Yuck, no."

"Sticker?"

"No. It's not going to happen. He and I—we *can't* happen."

"Why do love and romance have to be so hard to get?"

Bindi shrugged. "I think it comes in its own time, and if you miss it…"

"It's gone? For real?"

"Yeah, possibly. Don't squander it if you catch it. And that, guys and dolls, is the moral of our story." She smiled broadly, waved as Toya left with her son, then let the smile slip away and signaled for a waiter. She didn't order a steak, but went instead for dessert.

The decadent toffee dessert was devoured too soon, but she felt rejuvenated as she got up from the table to wash her hands in the powder room. She stepped away from her table but turned back when she realized she'd left the car seat. Snatching it up, she started back for the restrooms and halted to let a man and two women pass her. A long-legged woman with curly hair lighter and shorter than Toya's dropped her handbag.

A bottle with pills rattling inside rolled to Bindi's feet. She managed to pick it up. Prenatal vitamins. "Your vitamins?"

The woman turned with her hand out and took the bottle. "Thanks— Oh." Martha Blue, youngest daughter of the Las Vegas Slayers' new owners, was involved with a recently retired crazy-rich champion boxer. And she, according to her fat bottle of prenatal vitamins, had a bun baking in her oven.

The juicy tidbits were piling up in her lap—why hadn't she capitalized on any of it by now? Why was she having so much trouble going through the motions of the procedure that had for months satisfied her cost of living?

Saying nothing more, Bindi glanced once at the man and woman accompanying her—her parents, Marshall and Temperance Blue—and edged past them, lugging the car seat.

In the powder room, she set the seat on the counter and—

A gust of fragrant air preceded the drop-dead classy woman who entered the restroom on Bindi's heels and engaged the lock.

"Hey—"

Temperance Blue interrupted her with the iciest glare Bindi had ever seen in a pair of such warm brown eyes. "Bindi Paxton, before you get on your phone, we need to have a little chat. Go ahead as you were. I'll talk."

"Talk all you'd like. I'm out."

"Martha's pregnancy is a private matter, but you're going to exploit it for revenge or personal gain, just as you did when you launched that little media attack on my daughter Charlotte."

"Do you think I'm proud of everything I've done? Thirty years gives a hell of a lot opportunity to screw up. Did I take photos of Martha's pills? Nope."

"Gossip doesn't need proof."

"Credibility helps." Bindi proceeded to wash her hands, and by the time she was done lathering, rinsing and drying, she'd be done with this terse conversation. "Temperance, I am not a threat to your daughters."

"You're a threat to anyone who gets in your way," the woman retorted. "You and Alessandro Franco—"

"Are not of the same mind or body. His sins aren't mine, and I'm damn sick and damn tired of people linking me to what he did. Is this how you see Nate—as an extension of his father? The man's got balls of steel if he's committed to marrying Charlotte, knowing she comes with you and Marshall."

Temperance's white-gold bracelets gleamed under the powder room lights as her arms shook. "What did you say?"

*A whole heaping lot of stuff.* Bindi started for the hand dryer, but the other woman darted in front of her.

"You said 'marrying Charlotte.' Nate Franco—"

"Is marrying your daughter. His brother told me. Now ask yourself why I knew that before you did." Bindi gestured for Temperance to step back, and she continued drying her hands. "Your daughters don't seem the type to hold back, so I'm sure your nightmarish parenting techniques have already been pointed out to you. If I had a mother like you— Actually, I *do* have a mother like you, and she's in Illinois while I'm in Las Vegas. Connect the dots."

"Bindi, my daughters would never say that their fa-

ther and I don't love them. We don't always exist on the
same page, but my daughters are very much loved. If
they weren't they'd be harder, angrier—more like you."

"I'm loved." She wasn't but if she didn't lie, she'd cry.

"Have a good night, Temperance."

Bindi collected her stuff, unlocked the door and
walked calmly from the restaurant. And in light of Martha Blue's prenatal vitamins oops and Toya Messa's face-
to-palm divorce paperwork, she decided to rethink her
handbags, because if she was going to ever carry her secrets with her, she was going to carry them in a purse
that zipped.

Ten days after Toya's daylong disappearance, she was
gone again. This time to Iowa, with her baby, and Bindi
had seen them off in the airport. Afterward, she'd grudgingly acquiesced to a face-to-face meeting with Drew
Ross, who'd applied the pressure for an update. Until
the day before, she'd had nothing to report to him about
Alessandro Franco or Gian DiGorgio.

Standing at the counter of a downtown coffee shop,
Bindi had told Drew that Al still hadn't shown signs of
resurfacing. She thought it was far past jacked up that
the man who cared so deeply about bloodlines and lin-
eage was missing out on his sons' lives. He wouldn't see
Nate's wedding day. What if his heir apparent, Santino,
tied the knot?

She'd stemmed the thought, because as much as she
felt a private shiver of thrill to imagine him in a tux,
ready to make someone his, she couldn't maturely cope
with the reality that she wouldn't be his bride in white.

Men didn't love, honor or cherish her. She'd be setting
herself up for a well of hurt if she stuck her scratched-
up hopes on Santino Franco breaking the mold when he

was suspicious enough to have her followed out to the Indian Ocean.

Pushed and cornered, Bindi had passed along what Santino had told her about his father's expensive legal-god attorneys resigning as his counsel. It was all she had to give, and relinquishing even that seemed inexcusably wrong. Seeing Drew Ross absorb that information and give her a self-gratifying leer left her cold as she swept out of the coffee shop and into the cloudy afternoon.

She really wanted to cut, shape and create something. An unkempt hedge and a pair of shears would soothe her. Yet even if she did have access to shrubbery to tame and the topiary tools she'd put in a storage locker upon moving to her cozy, code for cramped, apartment, the approaching rain posed a threat. She needed something that'd stimulate and exhaust her.

She needed to make a call.

Holding off until she'd made it inside the quiet confines of her apartment, Bindi had given herself ample time to backpedal. So when she dialed a familiar number, she was couldn't say she was uncertain.

"Where are you?" she asked Santino, setting her phone on speaker and putting it on the mantel to free her hands.

"Working out."

Bindi paused midway, with her rain-touched shirt tugged halfway up her torso. So he was sweaty and his adrenaline was surging? She got rid of the shirt and licked her lips, but before she could inappropriately stroke her phone, she distracted her hands with tidying the coffee table. "How soon can you get showered and meet me for that dinner you impulsively suggested at Target?"

She pulled off her jeans, let them join the discarded shirt and waited.

"You booty-calling me, Paxton?"

"No. This is a *dinner* call." The bra hit the floor. It was *so* a booty call. An anything-he-could-give-her call. "Am I going to eat alone, or will you join me?"

"Where are your apartment buddies?"

"Toya and her kiddo are on their way to Iowa."

"Forty minutes. Let's go to Try Me, that burger place on the Strip."

That particular burger place was as upscale as they came in this city, and she'd have to break out the diamonds to blend in with the clientele. Funny thing about Try Me—you needed a thick skin or a dark sense of humor to appreciate its quirk, which was the serving staff's duty to write insulting comments on each patron's throwaway menu.

After meeting with Drew Ross's intentional offensive ways, she could handle Try Me's waitstaff. "Sounds like a d— I mean, sounds like dinner."

"Oh. I was thinking a date."

"A date." She grinned stupidly at her phone. "Yeah, a date. But let's make it an hour. I need to transform."

"From beautiful to what?"

Her smile fell at the word *beautiful*, but she didn't backtrack and undo the entire conversation. She just moved forward, because she was done going back. "See you in an hour."

An hour later, a pink strapless dress was hugging her and her dark hair was stylishly piled on top of her head to showcase her diamond raindrop earrings. Santino Franco was escorting her in a very unmistakable "hell, yeah, I'm with her. Got a problem with it?" way into a glittering black building with black-painted artificial trees tracing the perimeter. The interior was a blend of lust and luxury, with rap music swelling, and it reminded her of a password party for the rich and political that she'd attended several years ago.

"People are going to think we're a...well, a *we*," Bindi whispered to him as he banded an arm around her waist and they followed their waitress to a shiny black table. "I'm still Bindi Paxton. You're still Santino Franco. But keep your arm around me like this. I like it."

"I think you get a weird thrill out of confusing me."

"It's not weird," she said, smiling because she was weak to the temptation he and this place and her bubbling, excited, not-quite-broken heart presented.

As they sat opposite each other, the waitress eyed each of them, obviously recognizing them. "Complimentary tap beer, coming soon."

"Complimentary beer, eh? She must really want one of us." She winked.

Santino's face turned serious. "Bindi, I've been wanting you since I saw you walk past me at that Valentine's party on the island."

He'd had her, but clearly he wanted more. So did she. They needed to feed off each other. Whatever was building between them wasn't whittling away with each day they resisted touching and kissing and taking.

Oh, boy. This was getting out of control really fast.

"Is that really when? You can isolate the exact moment?" Not ready to go there, she attempted to steer the conversation back to light and playful.

Santino wasn't buying it. "I can isolate the moment I was ready to accept that I wanted you. If you're ready for more truth than that, tell me."

Bindi picked up her menu in answer. A new, less arousal-triggering topic was in order—the conversation equivalent of a cold shower. "My mother called me last week. I haven't called her back."

The waitress brought two beers, took their orders and sultrily walked off.

"Why did she call?" Santino asked her once privacy revisited them.

"She didn't say. If it was important, she would've sent certified mail or via an email." Daphne Paxton preferred to convey the tough things in the most impersonal ways possible. "This place should consider offering bowls of candy on each table. Nothing very special, but a few chocolates would be a nice touch."

Santino pushed aside his beer with a long, large-knuckled finger. "If a guy proposed to you offering a ring, and another proposed offering a two-pound box of chocolate candy, which would you say yes to?"

Bindi sat back against her chair. "I'd take the question seriously if you removed proposals from the scenario. It's not going to happen."

"So I should've asked which do you like better, rings or chocolate?"

"Rings don't make me feel euphoric," she answered honestly. "Chocolate does—has since I was about nine years old."

"Nine."

Santino didn't sound as intrigued as she expected he would. He sounded as though she'd echoed something he'd already known.

Of course. If he'd had her followed, he must've come across a little backstory. Aside from an unstoppable tic at her throat, she gave nothing away. "Nine years old. My parents said they'd teach me sweets moderation, but I think they were too busy being relieved that they'd weaned me off Valium. Do you suppose the burgers will be much longer?"

Santino covered her hands, but after a second she

pulled away. To let him reassure or comfort her tonight would feel like surrendering control she wondered if she had to begin with. "Not many people can come out on the other side of hell, Bindi. Do you want to talk about this?"

"No, I'll save that exciting conversation nugget for the next date."

"I want that—the next date and the chance to talk about the Valium."

"Santino, listen, it's not a drawn-out struggle. I was a problem child. I had issues that my parents had difficulties coping with, and they gave me Valium when I was about seven years old. It was for sleepaway camp, but they figured it worked so effectively, why not let me continue to take the pills as needed. 'As needed' turned into a routine, and my mom told me to never, ever forget to take a dose." Bindi pushed aside her menu as he had his beer. "One morning I couldn't remember whether I'd take my dose or not and I didn't want to see her upset, so I took what I needed and didn't realize until I started to get ill that I'd taken too much. I'd forgotten."

"Your parents shouldn't have given Valium to a kid."

"My mother told me she's sorry." *Sorry that she's my mother.*

"Bindi."

She gazed across the table at him. His fingers touched hers tenderly and brought her a little closer to true comfort, something her hard life had told her to stop believing existed for her. "Lots of men wouldn't want to stick around after hearing that, Santino."

"I said I'd protect you. That means staying with you through the messed-up shit, whether it's in the past or waiting around the corner."

*Oh, yes.* Bindi was nearly certain her ovaries had said that, instead of her always-on brain. Every particle of her wanted a say-so in what would happen after they left the restaurant.

When they ran through the drizzle of rain to her apartment building some time later, she decided she couldn't predict what would unfold, but she knew exactly what she wanted out of her time with him.

"Santino," she said when she shut the door to her apartment, secured all the locks and joined him near the sofa, "I want to know something. And I can't know it by having you say yes or no."

"Go," he encouraged, spreading his arms, and she used that opportunity to rush him. Knocking him back a few steps, she aligned her mouth with his.

"I need you..." Bindi lost her words in their kisses, worked her fingers through the short braid at the nape of his neck. Massaging his scalp, moving her hands across his shoulders to the bottom of his shirt, she got worked up and impatient and breathed a frustrated sigh against his mouth. "Please take off the shirt. Nothing else."

He lost the shirt, revealing the abstract tattoos that dressed him from shoulders to wrists. Bindi touched the cross on his right biceps, studied the word artistically written inside the intricate pattern. *Gloria.* He'd had his mother's name tattooed on his arm.

As Bindi was perilously close to dissolving into tears at the sweetness and sadness of his way of honoring his mother's memory, she directed her attention to his splendid body. *This* was beauty—a male body battered through a violent sport but reconditioned and made stronger.

Pointing to the pole, now naked of holiday lights, thanks to her roommate's insistence that it was ridic to leave them up past New Year's and her duty to make it right, Bindi said, "Stand in front of that. Line up your spine to it if it'll help."

"Why?"

"Because I need you to lock your hands behind your back—" she guided him, taking his wrist in order to bring one solid arm back and use the other hand to wrap around the wrist she held "—and control yourself. That's what I need to know tonight, that you can control your urges and sacrifice for me. Can you give me control when I need it?"

"I can do that for you, Bindi," he said in a quiet promise.

"I have to see it," she said. "So I need you to not touch me until I say it's okay."

Bindi moved the coffee table until it was directly in front of him, yet a few safe feet away. She got rid of her earrings as she stepped out of her shoes. "What do you want from me, Santino?"

"Loyalty," he said automatically. "I want to know you think about me."

"I do," she said, and the honesty hurt. She took down her hair, shook it free and turned away from him as she unzipped her dress. It dropped, and she stepped out of it and her panties, then sat on the coffee table. "I *have* thought about you."

"When?"

"Before you say you knew you wanted me," she said, boldly watching his body tense as he registered her erotic confessions. "I thought about you when it was so wrong to do it. I thought things I had no right to think. I dreamed it all, because I wanted to be...*faithful*."

"To him?"

Him. Alessandro. Neither could say the name, and that made them both cowards. "You not liking me then made dealing with the dreams easier. I could shut them down." She leaned back, spread her legs.

"Wider."

She could give him that, but first— "When did you first want me? I don't mean when you first accepted it."

"When he brought you into the house and you were everywhere. *Everywhere*."

Could they leave Alessandro in the past and take a hesitant step forward? "What did you want, Santino?"

"To have you naked, just like that. To be man enough for you."

Bindi opened her legs farther until she heard him groan. She touched herself, cupping her breasts, sucking two fingers into her mouth and gliding them into her already wet center. Watching him, she pleasured herself until she broke in front of him. Then sighing, shuddering, she went to him.

"I want you," he said over and over as she unfastened his pants and stroked him. "But, Bindi…"

She squeezed and coaxed, but the hardness she'd need to ride him was still dormant. There was too much interference in his head, and it almost broke her heart that she couldn't be the one to help him with that right now. "It's okay," she told him, easing her hands up his chest and kissing his mouth. "It's all right. This won't be what ends us."

Bindi gave him permission to drop his arms, and the first thing he did was bring her down to the sofa to hold her. And later, even though he was the one to console her, he fell asleep in her arms.

He wasn't the first in the past few weeks to be drawn to her for peace. First a baby drifted asleep in the crook of her arm. Then her friend had concluded her cry-fest by slumping against Bindi's shoulder. Now Santino Franco, a big, tough brute of a man, had found her safe to literally sleep with.

That made her either boring or comforting. With a little smile, she closed her eyes. She'd be happy with either one.

A man could sense when he was no longer welcome on the doorstep of a friend. It came in glimpses or like the puff of a changing wind. At times intuition attacked with a fist. Alessandro wasn't about to publicly recognize Tonio as a friend. Their fathers' falling-out had dictated that. Now in their sixties, both men had sons who were old enough to be fathers themselves. Tonio's son had died mixed up in a drug cartel in Colombia, and now he relied on his daughter to carry on his name and fortune and the consequences of his mistakes. Alessandro's sons would survive the adversity of having him as their father. Because they were Gloria's sons, too.

Gloria's blood ran through their veins, but her spirit stayed with him. It gave him the will to face another long day of hiding in Tonio's fishing-village market. It also bore down on him to the point that he sometimes had to lie down with his eyes open, staring at the cracked and sagging water-damaged ceiling of his room.

Today she was disappointed in him. He'd heard her spirit whisper as anyone would hear the determined buzz of a fly. Tonio wanted him gone, Gloria warned. He'd stayed so long that he'd become a liability.

On guard, Alessandro had come downstairs to the kitchenette at dawn to roll out dough, as Tonio had requested yesterday. His chore list came the day before they were expected to be complete. Each day of perfection— and staying out of the way of business—earned him another day in this crumbling safe haven. A card dispute with Tonio and some others, men Alessandro didn't know and should never have met, had almost found him on the other side of the door and fending for himself without a plan. The wedding band he'd now never see again had bought him dubious forgiveness. *Bastardos.*

Rolling the dough with the pin and shaping it with his flour-dusted hands, he kept his head down and his focus half on his Gloria, who looked after him. He couldn't see her dark skin and ready smile, but he could remember how cold her hand was a few years ago when over a hundred people had come to kiss his grandfather's ring, which he'd then put on her finger so that she could hold on to part of his treasure until they met again.

His sons had cried soundless tears for their mother. He'd howled and prayed, and at the lowest point he'd thrown his rosary away but found it again when he realized his money could do nothing.

Now he was alone. Grunting, moving a circle of dough to a tray, he went back to his task. That was the damn thing. There came a point, toward the end, when you found yourself utterly alone.

The aloneness made him worry about what he'd do next. Gian DiGorgio hadn't sent word in days, but the man was his friend so he need not worry.

But he did worry, every time Tonio cut his eyes at him or someone who knew trampled through the kitchen and muttered in Italian about strangers and treachery.

The kitchen was hot. He lifted an arm to rub across the sweat sticking to his forehead. How would he get out of this place?

The door opened and boots hit the flour-sprinkled floor. Alessandro did his chores, but not always cheerfully or neatly.

Wiping the sweat again, he looked up at the dark-clothed man. Not an Italian or one of the Colombians

Tonio had brought through a few days before. An Arab or an Indian? Either way, he was an intruder.

Springing back, Alessandro snatched up a knife.

The man smiled patiently. "Alessandro Franco, I'm wearing a Glock but didn't pull it. Would you set the knife down so we can talk?"

"Tonio's not here."

"I know." He offered a rough, brown hand to shake, but Alessandro kept the knife steady and tight. "I'm Zaf. I'm your only chance of getting out of this. This hiding place and your troubles in Nevada. Now put the knife down."

Gloria's encouragement tickled his ears, and he set the knife on the counter, the handle pointed toward him.

"Now I need you to do your part, Franco."

"What part?"

"You and Gian DiGorgio caused a lot of problems. You boys are keeping me busy untangling it all."

*"Fanculo."*

"That hurts, Alessandro." Zaf edged closer to the counter. "Save your vulgarities for this."

He stayed behind the counter but looked at an image on a smartphone as large as his palm. "Is that…Bindi?"

"She dyed her hair dark brown. *Back* to dark brown. Did you know her real hair color?"

Alessandro shook his head.

"Franco, Franco. You were going to marry her and you didn't know her real hair color?" Zaf wagged a finger at him, and Alessandro felt his face reddening with insult.

"I wasn't," he said to Gloria. He felt her behind him.

Zaf responded, "But you trusted her to hold down something for you on Cora Island, didn't you? Tickets for a flight out or—"

"Money. My money."

"There's no money. Bindi Paxton closed her account

on Mahé on February 15. Where did you tell her to put the money?"

Alessandro frowned. His eardrums hurt. His mouth was dry. Over two million euros… "The money. I didn't tell her anything, but she was supposed to stay on the island for two weeks. She—she was supposed to love the island. The water is cerulean. She swims like a fish and she likes jungles and—"

"Who's this man?" Zaf swiped the screen to show him a photo of his son. "Santino. What was he doing there? I'm thinking Bindi." Another swipe, and the photo battered Alessandro in the gut. Santino kissing Bindi.

Alessandro closed his eyes against the photo. "Enough, damn it."

"The same person your son recruited to keep an eye out for you made sure I could keep an eye on your son. In these situations, I'm usually the top bidder for loyalty." Zaf fiddled with the phone. "Your money's gone. The woman you proposed to is in Las Vegas with your son. Alessandro, come on. If you can't trust your son, who can you trust?"

He was faintly aware of the phone dinging. Recording. But he didn't care. He was numb. His mouth worked, but his voice had failed him.

"Can you trust your family?" Zaf coaxed. "Just tell me the truth, and then you can rest. I know you're tired. Let go of the burdens and you can rest, Alessandro. Now… can you trust your family?"

"No."

"Can you trust Tonio or Gian?"

"No."

"Look right here at the lens—" Zaf's face was cool, empty "—and tell me about Gian DiGorgio."

# *Chapter 9*

Santino had championship victories, versatility on the field that had contributed to stellar career reception records and an impressive profile from his rookie season through his final game, which had ironically taken place in his hometown. Fourteen years of superb on-field performance, colored by a penalty record that was indicative of his intensity and temper, had brought Santino far in life. But he had unfinished business in the NFL. The retirement dinner held in his honor hadn't felt like finality—more like an interruption or a pause.

Staring down the barrel of March, his agent had reviewed a promising prognosis from Santino's physiotherapy team and had begun circulating: phone calls, casual lunches, a few parties. He'd reported back that Arizona had a stable offense to start next season, so the likelihood of Santino returning to their roster had low probability. He had accepted that, wished the team well, and then his agent had cracked open a bottle of Absolut and said that if he wanted to get back onto the field, he had to be willing to leave the West Coast to do it.

It wasn't something Santino had right off considered—not with his father still missing and ongoing investigations rattling the foundations of every sector of his life. His brother could maintain emotional distance, and

Santino envied him that. Duty held him hostage, and he wouldn't know closure until he confronted his father and saw him take accountability for his greed and betrayal.

And then there was guilt. Santino had witnessed the fall of his father's relationship with Bindi, had known from the start that it wasn't one built on love, but he needed to face his father, man to man, and tell him that *he* was with Bindi.

He and Bindi were drifting together, not aiming toward the clear milestone relationship he'd had with Tabitha and not assigning definitions to what they were coming to mean to each other. But he was seeing her often, talking to her more, thinking about her with a constancy that made him feel centered.

Going into a late meeting at his physical therapy clinic, Santino had sent her a text message.

My place tonight?

Bindi had right away replied, Only if I can bring s'mores.

Grinning, he'd pictured her saying those words with that matter-of-fact expression and spark of sarcasm in her voice that got him too friggin' hot, and had answered with Got the ingredients from last week.

She'd brought them, but they hadn't gotten past opening the box of graham crackers before they'd tumbled onto the floor and made out as though that night would be their last.

Striding into the clinic, he went to the evaluation room where he was scheduled to meet with a physiotherapist, his primary-care physician and DeAngelo Bryant, his sports agent. He was expecting concrete finalized clearance that he was ready to return to the field. Once he had possession of that, word would filter throughout the league and the media, and his inspirational comeback would save him.

DeAngelo greeted him with a handshake and the others nodded solemnly.

No one was smiling.

"We're going to get right to it," his physician, Doctor Somner announced, assembling reports and bringing up images on a computer. "The existing nerve damage, while slight, is too vulnerable to re-injury in a contact sport, Santino. Your previous surgeries were unquestionably successful, and the consequences of your damaged intervertebral spinal disk are minimal, considering the impact of the hit and your age."

The words echoed around Santino's head. His body felt like ice. After everything he'd done, everything they'd said…they couldn't possibly…

The physiotherapist chimed in, "Your physical condition overall is incredible, especially for a man who's endured fourteen seasons in such a demanding offensive position. You're thirty-eight years old…"

"I have another season left," he protested.

"It's too risky, not only for your quality of life, but for an NFL team," Doctor Somner said. "The flexibility of your spinal disks have already begun to deteriorate with the aging process. That's a basic fact. Despite how well you maintain your body, the aging process continues. No debate—you look better than you ever have. You *look* like textbook physical fitness. Anyone seeing you without knowledge of your prior injury would jump at the chance to sign you up. But your spine's been compromised to a point where paralysis is your number one threat."

He'd practically tasted this victory, and now it was gone. Just like that. "What the hell happens next?"

"You're young—"

"But too old to receive a football," he grunted.

"Listen to them," DeAngelo said. "We knew it was a possibility that the comeback wouldn't happen. We wanted this for you, but…I'm sorry."

"You need to establish control of what *can* be changed," his physician continued. "The quality of your life is up to you. You've put this off before, but I'm recommending a urologist and a sexual therapist. Coming to terms with erectile dysfunction is going to help you regain your confidence."

"A man doesn't need sexual confidence to play football."

"He needs it to maintain sexual health."

"I'm capable of having sex. Hard-ons. Ejaculation. It happens."

"Inconsistently, right?" Doctor Somner challenged. "Is your decision to not pursue treatment options something you've discussed with your partners?"

"There's just one," he said, thinking of her and wanting to do more for her even though she insisted that she could handle his scuffs. "She said she's okay with it. She's resilient like that."

"*Resilient* doesn't sound like Tabitha," his agent commented.

"It's not Tabitha. I never had with her what I've got going with—" He stopped himself, right on the brink of screwing up. "With the woman I'm seeing now. She keeps me guessing, gives me peace of mind. She knows she's sexy, but she can't see how completely beautiful she is. She's okay with my problems."

"Damn," DeAngelo said, looking around at the other men. "You have a woman like that and you're keeping her name in the vault? I wouldn't."

*Would you, if she was a woman who was engaged to your father?*

Santino redirected the conversation to his dead career. He'd revive it or reincarnate it. He couldn't let himself take a walk with despair and give up. He wasn't *that* similar to his father. "I want to open the discussion for alternatives," he said to DeAngelo.

"I'm glad you said that. You're not getting back into a jersey and helmet, and you don't want the suit-and-tie desk job. You want a place in the NFL, on the turf."

"It's where I'm supposed to be."

"So hear me out—this is million-dollar advice. You were a leader in offense and you pushed your men for fourteen seasons. You're smart and Jimar Fray's hit didn't scramble your eggs. I'm confident that your chances of returning to the game have just reversed, if you're open to coaching."

*A coach—him, now?*

A half hour later, Santino drove to his place, split between defeat and optimism. His career as a player truly was over. The reality sank in slowly as he entered his condo, turned on the electric fireplace and sat on the sofa. Was he capable of channeling his passion for the game into an ability to direct his men on the field? Or would he live vicariously through them and always feel deprived of a dignified retirement?

Would he move forward or remain a prisoner to the past?

When he heard keys rattling outside the door, he quickly straightened up and tucked away his despair. A moment later, Bindi breezed into the room carrying a gift bag. "Last week I was looking around and decided your place isn't green enough." He'd bought the condo furnished, hadn't been interested in pretending it would be a real home. There was a total of one plant. "So I brought you something low maintenance to get you started."

He had to force himself to look away from her beauty, her infectious optimism, and opened the bag to find a Chia Pet inside. "A pig," he said, his mood lifting even higher despite himself.

"The pig is my favorite, so by default…" She shrugged, smiled, straddled him. "Do you hate it?"

"No, I don't hate it. Or detest it. Or dislike it." He kissed her cheek, lips, the side of her neck, and he got nice and comfortable there. He'd come to rely on her cottony-clean scent and how she moaned when he stroked a hand down her neck and held her still for his kiss.

"C'mon," she said, shoving aside the gift bag and dragging him to his bedroom. Quickly, she stripped down to her panties and fell playfully onto the bed. Her skin contrasted alluringly with the dark blankets. "Now come here beside me."

Santino lay next to her, lifted her arms above her head and ran a hand from her hip to her armpit, then back down again to turn her onto her side, facing him.

"Hey," she said, the word barely a breath, "you seem kind of stormy. You okay?"

"It's football. I'm not going to play again."

"Yeah, you're retired. I don't understand."

"I was in training this past year. I wanted a comeback."

Bindi's chin dropped, and she looked up at him through her lashes. "That explains the body. Training for a comeback? To Arizona?"

"Anywhere—at least that's what I was thinking. But it's been confirmed that the injury and my age aren't going to make it a safe bet. No team's going to want the risk."

"What about the risk to you? ESPN played the footage from that game against the Slayers nonstop. It was awful. I wouldn't want to see you on the ground like that again, ever. Am I right when I say you don't need the salary?"

"It's not the money, Bindi. It's about getting back what was stolen."

"Sometimes when we lose something, it really is gone. You take too long to accept change, and I'm the same way. You're not a football player anymore. Get over it." She smiled encouragingly. "I'm not in my twenties anymore. I'm getting over it."

She was frank and sweet and she was right. "My agent suggested I open up to other possibilities. Coaching."

"I think your agent is a very smart dude." Then, serious again, she kissed him. "I'm figuring out that people should try to open up to things that might be a better fit as they change. You couldn't play forever."

"I wanted to change the way I left the NFL."

"Nothing's going to erase the fact that you were injured and can't suit up again. So maybe your comeback will be different—I don't know, coming back in a different role. You have the technical skills. You were in line to inherit a franchise."

She was making too much sense, and making him see his stubbornness for the self-defeating roadblock that it was. "What about you and me, Bindi? We weren't right for each other when we met."

She made a noise of agreement. "We were chasing the wrong things. Now I'm different and you are, too. So we're…hmm…a better fit. A good fit. A matching set."

"Lock and key."

Laughing, she said, "Precisely. So are we going to keep doing this? Seeing each other?"

"We can keep doing what feels right."

"I like that idea." Bindi started to wiggle down, and then she was curled at the foot of the bed, snuggled against him and perfectly positioned to undo his fly. Stroking his shaft, she put her mouth on him.

Looking down, he smoothed her hair back and watched her suck him in as far down as she could. He felt his balls tightening, knew he was hardening as she touched him.

"Wait for me," she told him, using her hand to pump as she straddled his thighs and scooted into position. Her other hand clumsily tried to pull the crotch of her panties aside and she attempted to rock onto him—

But he felt the tension in his flesh ease, and, swearing, he said, "It's not going to happen. I wanted this to happen for us."

"It's all right," Bindi said after a moment, moving her hands up his chest and lying on top of him. "It can't always be the way we had it on the island."

"My doctor recommended a urologist and sex therapist. I haven't wanted to go that route because I know where it'll lead—to a point where I have to swallow down a pill every time I want to get close to you."

"A PDE inhibitor could work. Wouldn't you want to know if there are infertility problems?"

"Sounds as though you've been doing some personal research."

"I have," she said firmly. "I'll cop to that. Because I'm worried about how it's affecting *you* to not being able to perform the way you want to. I don't need PIV sex every time, all the time. I need to know that something can take off the pressure and let you concentrate on what you feel and who's making you feel it."

Bindi Paxton would fight this fight with him? How

could he have loved someone who didn't have her guts and persistence?

"There are workarounds. Sex isn't the only way to make love."

"Which are we doing, Bindi?" he asked, even though he was as ill prepared to answer the question as she.

The doorbell rang, and had his body not turned against him, he would've ignored it. But since he'd backed them into a corner with that question, he was only too relieved that Bindi slid off him so he could get up.

Zipping up, he went to the door. His brother was on the other side, and instead of waiting to be allowed inside, Nate swaggered in.

"Charlotte's in the car. We're taking you clubbing tonight. VIP access—"

"Thanks, but I'm going to hang back tonight," he said.

"That's sad as hell." Nate was about to say more, but he looked past Santino and narrowed his eyes at the purse on the leather sofa. "You have somebody here?"

"Yeah, I do." As Santino pushed the purse farther back on the sofa, he bumped one of the key chains and it released a mechanical meow.

"A cat key chain? The thing's eyes just shot out beams."

"I, um, think it's a flashlight key chain. You know, that meows." Shrugging, turned around and met the angriest look he'd even seen on his brother's face.

"Whose purse is that? How many women do you kick it with who have cat flashlights hanging off their bags? I know only one woman who's into novelty stuff like this. *One.*"

It appeared that the laser-eyed cat was out of the bag, and Santino saw no other route other than to own up the truth. "It's Bindi Paxton's purse."

"Are you doing Bindi? What the…?" Nate grabbed his head, let go, swore. "What the hell is happening to our family? Dad's been missing for a month and now you're having sex with his ex-fiancée? That's not right."

"Actually," interrupted Bindi, stomping across the dark wood floor, dressed in her top and pants, but obviously missing her bra, "we were in the middle of having sex, but now I'm going to make s'mores."

Nate averted his eyes. "Man, tell her to put something on or I'm going to give her my jacket."

Bindi shook her head and vanished into the kitchen.

"Nate, this wasn't some scheme. We're not together to hurt you or get back at Dad. I want Bindi in ways I didn't even want Tabitha. She knows me, Nate. Really, she knows me and she's with me."

"What's in this for her?"

"We're not together on a deal."

"So all of a sudden, after being enemies, y'all are lovers?"

"She was in the Seychelles on some trip Dad let her plan a while back. I went looking for her because I thought she might know where Dad went. She didn't know, but she agreed to come back to Vegas with me in case he tried to make contact with her."

Nate glanced warily at the kitchen and lowered his voice. "Sounds off—the fact that he didn't have the trip canceled when he broke things off. Can you trust her, Santino?"

"I do trust her. I'll regret it later if I have to, but this is working for us."

He saw Bindi appear in the kitchen doorway, now wearing a plain apron over her see-through shirt.

"There's something you need to know. Then you both can make up your minds about whether or not you trust me. Al gave me a bit over two million euros to keep in a deposit account on Mahé. He's always been a big spender, and he'd told me that we were going to be married by the time of the vacation, so I really didn't think it was all that odd." She looked at Santino. "The day after Valentine's, I emptied the account and had it closed. I donated it to a conservation society in the Seychelles. It can be verified. I didn't want to take any of it back with me."

"Two million," Nate said, shaking his head in disbelief. "That much money? It sounds like storage."

"Why didn't you tell me he'd had you put that much in the account?" Santino asked her, his mind whirling as these new puzzle pieces started to come to light. *Storage*, Nate had said.

"I thought it was ridiculous that Al would use me and a Valentine's vacation to get himself out of Dodge. And I didn't know if you really had my back. We had sex, but we didn't put all our cards on the table. So does that answer your question?"

Nate cringed.

"After I found out somebody disabled the security system at the villa, I didn't feel all that safe and decided I should leave."

"It was disabled?" Damn, he'd accepted that she'd simply forgotten to set it. He should've been on sharper alert. How else had her privacy been compromised on that island?

*Besides you going out there with her entire history memorized.*

"Yes, completely unarmed. So I checked out, emptied that account and…" She lifted her hands, dropped them. "I still think you're off about his plans. It's been a few weeks since then and he hasn't tried to contact me."

"Nate?" someone called out, knocking before pushing open the door. Charlotte Blue walked into the condo. "Santino, are you coming with us to— Bindi Paxton?"

Bindi waved, and looked to him to explain.

But Nate beat him to it. "Let me catch you up, Lottie."

"No, really, I think I can figure it out." Charlotte turned on her heel. "We should leave, Nate."

"Congratulations on the engagement," Bindi said to the pair. "Santino told me a couple of weeks ago. I didn't leak a word of it to anyone. So yes, Nate, to answer your earlier question, he can trust me."

Without a backward glance, Nate and Charlotte left the condo. Santino walked to the still-open door and hesitated. "Are you leaving, too, after going through that grilling?"

Bindi ran to him, kissed him hard on the lips. "You defended me to your brother. He's all the family you have left right now, and you faced him down to defend me." She hugged him. "Why don't we open up your new pig plant? It's not an expensive night out with VIP access, though."

"I don't need VIP access to anything but you, Bindi."

"ESPN's legal analyst is on, talking about Alessandro Franco."

Bindi, who'd been inspecting the leaves on her windowsill plants, set aside her magnifying glass and gardening kit to follow her roommate's voice, which was absent of its usual singsong cadence. Perched on an arm of the living room sofa, Toya held her son against her chest and tipped her head toward the television.

"Breaking news."

"Did they find him?" Bindi made a motion to clear the coffee table of its usual accumulation of designer accessories, baby toys, dishes and books and plenty other random things her friend touched on a daily basis, but it'd already been cleared. Not only cleared, but cleaned and lemony-fresh polished. Preoccupied, she sat on a corner of the table and listened to the analyst sandwiched between two sports anchors speak while she quickly read the information scrolling across the ESPN Bottom Line.

"…FBI has confirmed that Franco's former legal counsel is cooperating within the confines of the confidentiality agreement he signed last year. Attorneys Chuck Constant and Waylon Spencer are expected to issue a statement by the end of the week addressing the unauthorized release of call records allegedly between Franco and former Las Vegas Slayers defensive lineman Jimar Fray. A representative of the firm has acknowledged that this was an internal action, though it's yet to be confirmed whether or not the action was deliberate."

"Dammit," Bindi said, gnawing her bottom lip. "Former counsel. Did you catch the beginning of this, Toya? Did the analyst clarify whether someone in the office leaked the resignation decision as well as the records?"

"It was on, but I didn't hear everything until the name penetrated. This is really getting strange. The man's been missing for over a month. What about Gian DiGorgio? He's being hunted, too, isn't he?"

"No one has been able to get anything to stick without Al to give him up."

"How certain are we that this is a suspect-skips-town story? What if there was—" Toya craned her neck to give Bindi a sympathetic look through her cat's-eye glasses "—foul play?"

*Please, don't let it be that.* Alessandro Franco had treated her carelessly, and she wanted him to face the consequences of his illegal activities, his abuse of power as an NFL team owner and, particularly, his cruel choice to pay someone to injure his own son. She didn't wish him well, but she didn't wish him death, either.

She thought of Gloria Franco's name tattooed into a cross on Santino's biceps. Would he add his father's name, if...

Bindi stood up. "Toya, I need to go."

"Somewhere?" Though evidently concerned, Toya asked no more than that.

"Be home soon."

Bindi texted Drew Ross from the apartment building's parking lot, and this time she did meet him in his corner office. This would be their final meeting, and she would not be joining *The Vegas Beat*.

She wanted out. In the beginning she'd wanted security, a chance to find her footing in the workforce, but to find that security by betraying someone she cared about seemed irredeemable and as dirty as anything she'd ever done.

"What I told you about Alessandro Franco's lawyers dropping him—did you release that information?" Bindi asked, sitting across from him.

Drew, who hadn't done so much as to stand or signal her to enter the office, watched her wordlessly from his taller, wider chair. On that side of the desk sat the superior; on the other side, the inferior. "Walk around to this side of the desk, Bindi," he said, and his voice made her think of frost. "Look at *The Beat*'s home page."

Bindi did, and reviewed the new stories as he scrolled to the bottom and then to the top. "I don't see anything involving Franco."

"We didn't jump on it. At your request, I held off. I thought you could get me more. Now ESPN and some third-rate sports blogs have freakin' phone records. Did you know about the phone records?"

"No. I saw it on TV."

"What do you have for me? Give me something. I need a competitive edge here—everyone's on this now."

"I'm not doing this anymore, Drew."

"We have a deal."

"Not anymore. I don't want to be on your staff. I don't want to be a double agent, either. This is a real family we're targeting. I don't want to get a job this way."

"They're all celebrities. Collateral damage."

"Not to me."

"Is this eleventh-hour change of heart out of respect for Alessandro, or because you're letting his son screw you?"

Bindi put some space between them. "Don't talk to me like that."

"All right. You don't have to give me a straight answer." Drew steepled his fingers. "Just a word of advice. Every reporter knows if you got something to hide, you don't parade it around the city. Think about that the next time y'all want to go to Try Me together. Now get out."

Bindi couldn't say she minded all that much that people knew she was seeing Santino Franco. Caring about him, spending time with him, wasn't against any laws. The morality of their connection, the complexities of their relationship, was easy to judge but nearly impossible to genuinely understand.

Santino understood, and she did, and that was enough to fill her with strength and hope despite the turmoil she sensed was coming to a head.

Bindi was relieved to return to the tiny apartment that had, day by day, become a safe place for her. It had something to do with being used to seeing a baby crib in the living room and her friend's random stuff adding character all throughout the place. Toya herself was a safe place, someone to laugh with at the end of a long day, someone who left food crumbs on the counter but always set aside leftovers in fresh-lock containers, someone to consult on all matters of makeup and clothes.

And the baby… Oh, that baby had hold of Bindi's heart and wasn't going to let go anytime soon. She was all right with that.

Coming through the door, she wanted to curl up on the sofa and hug him.

She ventured forward, calling, "Toya-Toya-bo-Boya, I'm back," as she pursued the baby crib.

Only, it wasn't there.

Technically, it was, but it was dissembled.

"Toya?" Bindi stepped over the scatter of parts and the now-shrink-wrapped mattress, heading to the hallway. "Toya, what's going on with the baby's crib?"

Toya emerged from the bathroom with her son bundled in towels. "Hey, Bindi. Holden and I are moving out."

"Moving out?" The woman had swept in like a funnel cloud and was leaving the same way? "When—and why?"

"My parents asked me to come home to Iowa. When I visited, we had this amazing heart-to-heart, and they don't want Holden and me to stay so close to Asher right now. It's just too tangled with all these feelings and high emotions getting in the way of what's best for the baby. So we talked this morning and I said I would come home. They're arranging everything—the moving guys, the flight—and you're getting a basket! As a thank-you for opening your home to me. It should be here in a few days." Breathless, Toya smiled. "I didn't tell them about the stripper pole."

Bindi laughed. She was sure she'd cry first—a loud, all-out Toya-style bawl. "Save it for Thanksgiving con-

versation or something." She paused. "Does the leaving
ASAP have something to do with that ESPN breaking
news we heard today? My connection to Alessandro
Franco?"

"No," Toya said emphatically. "You are not involved
in that. I know it. Holden and I have been nothing but
snug-as-a-bug-in-a-rug safe with you."

"Okay."

"Oh, you. I'm going to miss you, girl."

"Me, too. It's so sudden. I have zero time to get used
to the idea of you and Holden leaving. I went and let myself get stuck on you guys."

"And that's okay. We're stuck on you, too." Toya offered the baby and Bindi took him, even though it'd hurt
that much more to let him go. "You're truly my friend.
You inspired me to get past losing Asher and the settlement. I'm going to be the most kickass Toya Keech I
can be."

"You gave up his name?"

"I did. Already filed the paperwork." Toya followed
Bindi to the living room. Funny, now that she knew her
friend was leaving, she could see the signs. Things put
in their place and clean, fewer toys scattered around the
apartment. "I decided to get Holden all washed and clean
before we take off. Want to help get him ready to go?"

Bindi almost said sure, but a half gasp, half sob
stopped her. She shook her head and went into the
kitchen. She needed a friend within reach when Toya
and her child left. Dialing Santino's phone, she did her
best to control her wobbling voice as she asked him if
he'd be free to come over tonight.

When he showed up under an hour later, just missing the moving men who'd loaded up the baby's bed and
taken the last of Toya's belongings, she was almost as re-

lieved as she'd been the first time he'd come to her apartment, carrying a car seat brand-new in its box.

Toya, on her way out with her baby wide-eyed and too cute to say goodbye to, stopped short when she saw Santino in the doorway. Turning to Bindi, she said, "He's the *someone*, isn't he?"

"He is."

Toya grinned slyly at Santino. "The way you looked at her gave you away in two seconds flat. Take care of her, okay? Try not to leave food crumbs on the countertop."

"Thanks for the heads-up."

"Always." Toya gestured for Bindi to join her in the hallway. "I cracked open my nest egg to give you something in appreciation for taking Holden and me in."

"Wait, the basket?"

"No, no, that's from my folks. There's an envelope on top of the refrigerator. I paid for you to attend a horticulture program. Very low commitment, and I thought you'd enjoy it. It starts next month, just in time for Arbor Day. Read the info in the packet and decide if you're interested. I just wanted to say thanks."

"Thank *you*," Bindi said, and there were the tears again. She opened her arms wide to hug Toya and the baby, and when they left, she went back into the apartment and sat next to her someone on the sofa.

"Since I don't want to think about the hell spinning around my family, and you want to get your mind off your friends, I had this idea."

Not sex. She wasn't in the frame of mind for it, and emotionally she needed a different kind of consolation. She would tell him no and see if he'd leave straightaway. Better to find out now than become even more tightly entwined with him. "What's the idea?"

Santino pointed at the television. "Madden NFL. The stuff's in my truck. Just say the word."

*Oh, yes. You're my someone.* "The word."

They hooked up the console, and even though Bindi struggled to grasp the functions of the game despite knowing her stuff when it came to actual NFL gameplay, she they kept at it until she finally admitted defeat. "I guess I'm not versatile," she said. "I'm outdoorsy. Topiary art and diving and exploring."

"You dive?"

"Yes. In fact, I did on the Seychelles. I have pics." She picked up her phone and selected the correct album. The first was a selfie of her in a wetsuit. Figuring he'd get bored after a few finger swipes, she got up for a bottle of water and left him to it. When she returned, she heard people speaking.

Her voice…and who was the male? Drew Ross.

"…why Alessandro Franco's golden boy would enlist you."

For a moment she went light-headed, hearing everything that had been good in her life tumble down. Bindi rushed to the sofa. "Give me the phone. You don't want to know this way."

Santino held the phone away, his face made of stone. "You didn't want me to know at all."

"Santino thinks his father wants to find me. He believes I have something Al wants."

"Give me the damn phone, okay?" She reached, and when she made contact, he let her take it away. "Santino, I ended that deal with him. He's a creep and he's shady—"

"Yet you had a deal with him to begin with." He stood up, walked around the sofa. "When did you end the deal?"

"Uh…"

"The truth. Just let yourself spit it out. Assuming you're even capable of it."

That hurt, but what could she say? "I ended it today, but I didn't tell him anything except what you told me about Alessandro's attorneys resigning as his counsel."

"Oh, the news that blew up every damn sports news station today?"

"Drew said his people didn't leak it, and he was pissed enough that I believe him. It had to have been the person from the law firm who also leaked the phone records—I never knew about those, so how could it have been me? He's a sleaze, but I don't believe his paper was behind this." She tried to come forward but he moved backward. "I'm sorry, Santino. I…I never meant to hurt you. Hurt us." She should have ended things with Drew a long time ago, and she could barely breathe around the regret.

"You said I could trust you, but you had an active side scheme going with that Ross bastard. Bindi…no. This isn't going to work. You won't let it work."

"*I* won't? I'm standing here listening to you tear me to shreds, and I'm waiting for you to finally admit that you had me tailed to the Seychelles. You didn't suddenly remember my Valentine's vacation. You had somebody find me, right? And they were so thorough, weren't they? Reporting to you that I brought along purple suitcases? And why weren't you surprised to find out what happened to me when I was a kid?"

"I'm not going to lie about it—yes, I knew. But I didn't search for you. A guy stepped to me with a file in his jacket, and it had your life on paper." He appeared repentant and unapologetic. How could that be? "I went to the Seychelles to find my father. That was my purpose, and it was why I was desperate enough to do what I had to do to find you. Yeah, I'd take the information if it meant getting to my father. Don't act like it's unimaginable."

Bindi shoved her phone into her jeans' pocket. "It pisses me off that you'd let me go on about how much I valued your honesty knowing you were lying to me. I only made the deal with Drew because I thought you were having me followed. All I knew at that point was that you appeared no different from the other men who used me. I was *protecting* myself."

"I had to do it to find my father."

"And I had to do what I did to get a job and support myself. That was the deal I had with Drew Ross. Why is what I did so much worse than what you did?"

Santino completely ignored her challenge. "You'd work for that asshole? After what he said to you? I'm angry with you right now, and I'd *still* hurt him to make him sorry he handled you like that."

Images of bloody fistfights surfacing on every tabloid's front page danced in front of her. "Stay out of it. I can handle scum like Drew, and I did. Like I said, the deal's over. And it sounds as if *we're* over." The words hurt more than she could have ever imagined, as though someone had reached inside of her and was methodically tearing everything to shreds.

"What were we before tonight, before I found that recording on your phone?"

"Friends. But my friends don't stay. So go."

"We were not friends. We were more than that, and you know it."

"Go," she said again, moving past him to open the door for emphasis. When he stormed out, she shut the door and it almost broke her.

She retrieved her phone again. How had people screwed up their lives before cell phones anyway? She didn't want to delete the recording for the very reason she'd recorded it to begin with. But she wished she and Santino had started off honest and whole, instead of self-protective and scarred.

No, that wasn't even true. She wished they could've started off honest in spite of being self-protective and scarred. But maybe that was impossible. Maybe it just wasn't meant to be, and the past they shared would always overshadow whatever they might have wanted.

She absently scrolled the recent calls. Her mother had phoned again, and once again she hadn't left a voice mail message. This time, Bindi dialed her back.

"What can I do for you, Mom?" she said when Daphne answered.

"We—Roscoe and I—have been thinking about you. A while ago you mentioned you were playing with the idea of visiting home?"

"No, I'd said I wanted to come home, and you clearly didn't find that a desirable idea."

"Oh." Daphne gently cleared her throat. "Bindi. Would you like to come home? Your father and I could accommodate you."

Here her mother was asking her to come back to Illinois, yet she was spinning it as though Bindi had called her for a favor. "Of course, Mom. I'd appreciate that. I'll see you tomorrow."

"Uh—*tomorrow*?"

"Yes. Warn Daddy." Bindi hung up, gripped her phone. And when she sank back into her sofa in her quiet Las Vegas apartment, there was no one to offer her a shoulder as she cried. She should be used to it, but now...now that she'd had her first taste of having someone be there for her?

She'd never felt so alone.

# Chapter 10

Alessandro prayed for sleep. With his rosary in his grip, he lay awake on the makeshift bed in his room above Tonio's market and stared again at the ceiling. Dulled and cracked, it looked tired. *He'd* been tired for so long that he no longer felt tired. His aged body had adjusted to the physical fatigue and mental weariness. He maintained strength to complete his chores, could eat his meals and appreciate liquor and partake in card games that continued to test his gambling abilities. But in the late hours, Gloria didn't come, and he missed her.

In the late hours, he could clearly recall what he'd done in the States and why he'd let Gian help him find an underground escape from the falling consequences. He recalled the events with as much lucidity as he had the afternoon that stranger—Zaf, was it?—had come to him with those photos of his son and his ex-fiancée. Alessandro had left Santino in such an angry state the last time they'd spoken. And Bindi Paxton… Alessandro hadn't known what to do with the woman's vivacious, ambitious spirit but to douse it. But that'd been a long time ago.

It made a strange sort of sense that Santino and Bindi would heal each other. A man didn't kiss a woman that way and mean nothing behind it. A woman didn't hold a man that tightly if she intended to immediately let him go. A couple didn't come together the way they appeared in the photos if there was no pull between them.

But it'd happened while Alessandro was preparing to go to the Seychelles and reclaim his money and Bindi. All she'd had to do was stay on her holiday, and once he'd found her, he would've been able to convince her to either come with him or silently watch him go.

Zaf, who'd reeked of an unspoken agenda, had been right.

*If you can't trust your son, who can you trust?*

Alessandro couldn't trust either of his sons. Nate had transferred his loyalty to his woman. Santino had touched Bindi Paxton. No…he'd fallen for her. It was all there in the photos.

There was no one to trust anymore. He couldn't trust himself to not get himself killed in a tiny Italian fishing village. Clarity faded in and out during the day, but it had felt terrifying and fortifying to recall and convey Gian coming to him with a business proposition when Gloria had died.

*The grief will pass when your percentage of the money comes in. The bigger the payout,* amico mio, *the less pain you feel.*

He'd taken the highest risks he could, had won a few hands, but soon the losses had begun to add up. Gian had guided his hands at every step, yet the man was free to operate his exclusive casino in Las Vegas, while Alessandro was here and praying for sleep.

In sleep, he would find Gloria. She was all he needed now, and as he sat up and let his gaze chase the shadows of the room, he began to mourn her again. Mourning hurt more than the fear that Gian would retaliate against him for talking to Zaf's camera. Gian wouldn't understand the beauty of unburdening oneself when the end of struggle was close enough to brush with your fingers. It was rapture.

Alessandro scratched his scraggly beard, slowly getting to his feet. The bed, one thin mattress stacked on top of another, groaned and complained. He walked on shaky legs to the door, opened it and took the stairs carefully into the darkness.

At the bottom, he started to turn on the lights, but someone else did it for him. Tonio had timed him right. Though the room was now illuminated, all of a sudden Alessandro couldn't see clearly.

"Gian DiGorgio wants you relocated in the morning," Tonio said, his breath rattling against the phlegm in his lungs working its way into his throat. He sat on a stool with a slab of luncheon meat within reach and his hands folded on his round belly. "I don't think you want that trip."

Alessandro briefly closed his eyes. The stranger named Zaf must've traveled back to the States and shown Gian the recording. He shouldn't have talked, but Gloria had been in the room and he'd wanted to explain how he'd become enfolded and engulfed in something he couldn't escape.

"Al…Al, come closer." Tonio reached up to fold his paws over Alessandro's shoulders. "He says you've been in Sicily too long. The woman you depended on left the island early, and when Gian checked on the account you claimed she had, he found out it was closed. There's no money. He can't take more risks for you. And he says you have information you can't be trusted to keep quiet about."

Apparently, Gian *didn't* know that Alessandro had talked. But he was having him "relocated" anyway.

"Gian's my friend," Alessandro whispered, bewildered.

"I want you to think about something tonight." Tonio nudged a tiny wrapped bundle across the counter. "Unwrap it."

Alessandro's fingers worked slowly, but finally he had the bundle open. A razor blade.

Tonio pointed to Alessandro's chin. "Clean yourself up. Run a bath. Make sure it's warm. Take a walk." The man got up and shuffled over to kiss his cheek once, briskly, then he waddled back to the door. "When you walk, go down the road. Don't cross the street."

Tonio left and Alessandro carried the blade upstairs to the little bathroom with the cracked mirror. He would shave, and Gloria would see him smooth faced with his hair dark. She might see the man she married, and her smile would brighten her lovely brown face.

Alessandro shaved carefully, going slowly to avoid nicking his skin. When he was done, he nodded and looked toward the stream of daybreak intruding on him. Bending toward the tub, he ran a warm bath.

He started to put on fresh clothes, a pair of shoes, to retain some sense of dignity. Yet his mistakes had drained any semblance of pride from his life, and he no longer deserved any.

Sitting in the warm water, he watched the water engulf his legs, and when he submerged his arms, the hair darkened against his tanned skin. Considering his arms, he pushed up his sleeves.

*Down the road*, Tonio had said. *Not across the street.*

Alessandro positioned the razor blade. And he thought of his sons.

A car was waiting at Chicago Midway International Airport to collect Bindi and escort her directly to her parents' sprawling Georgian-style house in the Highland Park suburb north of Chicago. She'd packed for a three-night stay—she couldn't imagine Roscoe or Daphne insisting that she linger any longer than that.

But she would enter their home with a positive outlook and faith in her heart. Because she loved her parents, despite their feelings toward her and their inability to mesh as a family during her formative years. Perhaps they'd gotten past their frustration with her, and that was why her mother had made efforts to contact her.

Bindi couldn't fight her smile as the luxury car slowed in front of the mansion she remembered. Oh, that was right. Once this had been *her* home, too.

She checked her makeup in her compact mirror. You couldn't tell that she'd cried last night over losing her friend to Iowa and then breaking up with her *someone*.

"I'll bring your bags to the servants' entry. Feel free to step out here, Ms. Paxton," the driver said in polite sternness. He didn't get out to come around the car and open her door to the March chill, but that didn't bother her.

The actual wintry wind that said hello the moment she stepped out of the warm private car? *That* got to her, penetrating her Burberry trench coat, which, accessorized with an umbrella, was all the real weather protection she'd needed for Nevada winters. Snow clung to bushes and tree branches that must be laden with fat leaves from spring through fall. Astonishingly, she didn't remember whether she'd ever climbed any of these robust trees. Pity if she hadn't. They looked perfect for a more youthful version of herself to climb.

Ten years was a long time to be away from home. Today she wore a deep gray midlength dress, stilettos, pearls and a pair of tortoise-colored sunglasses. She wouldn't be swinging and scaling her way up through the branches and limbs toward that pale blue sky. Too bad.

Clutching her sleek purse, she took the winding front walk fast, dodging spots of ice and playfully disturbing the snow-coated hedges she passed on her journey to the antique double doors.

Tessa, a maid who had been in her family's employ for as long as Bindi could remember, welcomed her cheerfully, taking her coat and complimenting her dress as she led her into the interior of the mansion. People cut across their path busily, barely sparing a glance in her direction.

"Am I interrupting anything?" Bindi asked Tessa.

"No, it's only your father's campaign staff. Ignore them. It's what they prefer," Tessa confided.

The wide hallways and mahogany walls and the original artwork that her parents had proudly collected during her childhood all began to replace her optimism with trepidation. She should be excited to see her father and mother after ten years away from Illinois. Maybe it was because even though she'd called Daphne to update that she'd made it safely into town and was on her way, no one but a maid had greeted her at the door.

*They're busy people. It's not as if I gave them much of a heads-up.*

Bindi watched the maid step into a spacious room, speak with somebody then return to the doorway. "Welcome home, Ms. Paxton. Ask for me if there's anything you need during your stay. I'll go fetch your luggage. Mrs. Paxton already requested that we prepare your childhood room."

"That's fine." The formality had her palms feeling a bit clammy. "Thank you, Tessa."

Tessa gave her a friendly wink, then strode off.

"Come in," a strong, deep male voice commanded, and Bindi startled.

"Hi, Daddy," she said, finding him standing in front of a tall fireplace with two other men and a woman. Her mother, she realized, seeing that Daphne had allowed her dark hair to gray in silvery streaks throughout the short tresses. "Hi, Mom."

Daphne's gaze brushed her up and down. "Bindi, oh, get over here and hug your mother. I've never seen a more stunning woman."

Bindi hugged Daphne, then moved over to her father. The last time she'd seen him, he'd fired her from his campaign team and she was packing suitcases in a big dramatic scene that had left household staff in tears as they'd begged her to reconsider.

Illinois Democratic Senator Roscoe Rayburn Paxton hadn't appreciated being outed as unfaithful to his wife, which Bindi herself had been instrumental in seeing happen. She'd known about the affair, and when she'd tried to tell her mother, Daphne had shushed her and reprimanded her for saying such a thing without proof. So Bindi had obtained video proof and had had it publicly leaked so that even if Daphne refused to believe her, the general public wouldn't.

Her father faced her in a crisp suit with an American flag pin stuck to a lapel. His dark skin creased with shallow wrinkles she didn't remember him having the last time she saw him. Still, he had that strong, confident jaw, short and wavy hair and secret-seeking eyes. "Bindi."

"Hi, Daddy," she said again, taking off her sunglasses to look him in the eye.

Roscoe banded his arms around her and she went gratefully, sighing into his chest because she could hear his heartbeat and it'd been much too long since she'd known either of her parents' embraces. "How long before Las Vegas calls you back?" he asked her.

"I brought enough clothes for a few days," she said, almost adding that she'd travel home again soon if he and Daphne wanted her back as family. If they could just try again...

"Roscoe, you have eternity with her. She's your girl. What about the rest of us old fools?" someone said, and she leaned back to see Mort Jeffries, one of her father's longtime friends.

"Uncle Mort!" She pecked his grizzled cheek.

"What? No, kiss me like you mean it."

Everyone laughed gently and Bindi gave him a noisy smooch.

"What are you doing with yourself now, young lady?" Mort asked, cutting his eyes at her parents. "Roscoe—Daphne—you're supposed to keep an eye on your only child. Don't let her stay away for another ten years."

Daphne stood beside her. "Bindi's very much a part of our lives. In fact, we'd like to include her in Roscoe's presidential run."

*Presidential...what?* Bindi shook her head. This had to be jet lag playing tricks. Her father had resigned from Congress when she was in college, shortly after the cheating scandal had jarred him out of the public's favor. No longer America's "Boy Scout," he'd stepped back from politics and, the last she'd heard, was focusing on backing organizations he believed in and improving his squash game.

"You're organizing a presidential campaign, Daddy?"

"I am, Bindi. It's time to return to politics, to get in front again. I have very influential supporters and I managed to twist Mort's arm to head up the campaign. Mort's campaigns are winners. His candidates have never lost. True fact," he said with a grin toward his friend.

"I thought you were done with politics, though," she said, still confused. She didn't like the pressure senatorial races and councilmen races had put on him, the strain it had applied to the Paxton family, the role she'd played in helping her father succeed. "You and Mom are supposed to be enjoying your retirement."

"I'm a volunteer," Daphne piped up. "Three museums in the city."

"And I'm always going to be a politician. Welcome home, Bindi. Let's get you oriented with what we're doing."

Surprised that she hadn't been released to visit her bedroom and unpack, Bindi took a seat in the office. Everyone else continued to stand.

"My platform is diversity," her father announced in his booming vibrato.

"Really? Mom converted to Christianity and stopped speaking to Grandma because Grandma kept insisting that she and I would always be Jewish. You, Daddy, insist on identifying as African-American even though you're multiracial."

The others glanced around. A few people cleared their throats and someone whispered, "You said she wouldn't be problematic."

Daphne came closer. "Bindi, I know you didn't take it especially well when my ma died and she and I had all those hurt feelings between us. But she loved you and was so grateful that you wanted to maintain a connection to her. You have her dreidel still, don't you?"

"I do. I have everything that reminds me of where and who I come from."

"Perfect. You're the face of the...the new average

American, Bindi. Your father would be in an excellent position should you work with him on this campaign and show your support for this family."

"And if I don't cooperate with something I'm hesitant to believe in?"

"Bindi, politics is about gray areas," her mother said gently. "You want to see your father succeed, don't you? You love your daddy, don't you? He depends upon you and I to back him up. I need your help."

Bindi swallowed, her throat tight. "I'll think about it. But did you call me because of this campaign assembly, Mom? Respect me enough to be honest, please."

"Oh, Bindi." Daphne laughed, as though it were absurd. "Oh, of course I called you because I was missing my daughter. You're number one in our lives."

Her heart, along with any last threads of hope about reconnecting with her parents, sank like a stone.

Bindi soon excused herself to freshen up and reacquaint herself with her childhood home. She encountered Tessa again and asked her to help her find the doors leading to the backyard. Wrapped in a stately black peacoat, Tessa accompanied her outside.

"What are you searching for?"

"My swing. Daddy designed it and had it constructed on the day Mom went into labor. Isn't that incredible? I've missed it, all this time…" Bindi stopped walking midway across the enormous yard and began to turn. "Where is it?"

"There is no backyard swing anymore, Ms. Paxton." Tessa puffed her breath against her linked hands. "I apologize. If I'd known that was what you were looking for, I would've told you before you walked out here in your lovely shoes."

Bindi cared little for her shoes when the swing—her

swing—was gone. "Uh, don't worry about it. It was just a silly childhood thing."

"Built the day you were born? To undo such a gesture," Tessa said, tsking.

"I really upset my parents, and if we're being fair, I haven't been home in ten years." *Because they never welcomed me back.*

"I'm sorry, Ms. Paxton. Would you like to go inside now?"

"Sure." Because if she stayed out here alone, she'd cry and the tears would freeze on her face. She couldn't let a swing break her composure. She joined the maid in the kitchen and was all too delighted to be able to stay in the cozy room listening to Tessa talk. The maid was as friendly as all the staff Bindi had known when she'd lived here before.

"I'm afraid your mother and I will be gone for a bit this afternoon. I'm accompanying her to her doctor's appointment."

"Is she okay?"

"Why, yes, she is. Menopause isn't easy to adjust to."

"Menopause?"

"Yes, she was officially diagnosed a few weeks ago. Poor thing. And she and Mister Paxton were so hoping for a child."

"A child?" *She* was their child. She was their idea of the face of the new average American.

Realization slapped her hard. "Mom called me after she found out she won't be able to have more kids."

"I can't speak to that," Tessa said, setting a mug of tea in front of her.

"Thank you, Tessa, but I'll pass on the tea. I really would like to speak to my parents." Bindi traced her way back to the office. Only Roscoe and Mort remained. "Where's Mom?"

"Not in here," Roscoe said, "but, Bindi, would you step inside for a moment? Shut the door behind you."

Bindi closed the door. "What is it, Daddy?" She noticed the television was on, the volume muted. Only after a double take did it sink in whose picture was featured on the screen. "Turn up the TV. Hurry. That's Alessandro Franco."

Roscoe raised the volume and the words *attempted suicide* grabbed her.

"Oh, God." *Santino.*

Roscoe turned off the television promptly. "That's not your worry anymore. You're here now. Mort's driving into Chicago for a late lunch. If you want to get reacquainted with the area, there's no better guide."

"No. I need to go to Las Vegas."

"There's nothing you can do for Alessandro Franco."

"I can be there for his son. We—we're close."

"Bindi," her father cautioned, "don't be rude. Mort has agreed to run my campaign. We owe him some hospitality."

Bindi's entire form stiffened. Both men watched her, and her mind slid back through the years. Age eighteen, at a political celebration in her father's honor.

"Mayor Dougal is a good friend," he'd said. "I give you permission to ride into the city with him. Be friendly, Bindi."

"Friendly" had meant willing, and she'd resisted, saying, "Daddy, he tried to kiss me. I'm not going anywhere with him."

In the end, her father had convinced her to take the ride and that she would be proud to have supported his career. When she'd come home late that night, she'd been dazed and so cold inside, and she'd passed a strange woman leaving. Inside, her father had been waiting in the study, his shirt more unbuttoned than it should've been, and he'd asked, "Bindi, were you friendly to Dougal?"

"Yes," she'd whispered, and she'd tried to hug him.

"Take a shower, Bindi."

"I took one before we drove back." She'd shivered. "I love you, Daddy."

"I love you, too. Go take another shower, and go to bed. Don't wake up your mother."

Dougal had been the first, but there'd been others over the next two years. She'd stopped feeling cold and had begun to feel nothing. Now, at age thirty, she was angry enough to stop a pattern that should have never started. "No," she said to both men. "I will not go into Chicago with anyone. Uncle Mort, you were like another father to me." She shook her head. "Nothing's changed."

"Bindi," her father began, "think rationally."

"You're disgusting." The anger built and built until she finally couldn't hold back the poison that she'd kept inside of her for so long. "Did all your politician friends report back to you about what they asked me to do and what they did to me? I should've fought you then, but I'm doing it now. Stay away from me—*both* of you."

The doors opened and Daphne entered with two other people wearing flag pins. "Bindi, have you started unpacking?"

"No, and I'm glad I didn't. I'm not staying. In fact, I'm leaving now. Daddy wants me to dole out favors to Uncle Mort, if you can see how messed up that truly is. And you, Mom, you don't have to stay with him and try to conceive another child to help out his presidential campaign."

Daphne's mouth worked like a fish out of water. "That's crazy."

"You don't believe me? That's fine. I know plenty of people in Las Vegas who will." Bindi faced glares from both parents. "Daddy? I wouldn't want a man like you to represent this country."

Feeling as though the weight of the world had been lifted off her shoulders, Bindi collected her luggage. No one followed her. No one stopped her as she marched out the door to the idling car outside, letting her childhood go for once and for all. "Take me back to the airport, please," she told the driver. "I'm going home to Las Vegas."

# Chapter 11

Santino and his brother monitored the hallway outside of Alessandro's room in shifts. Switching shifts with Nate meant battling a crowd of media outside the Las Vegas hospital where Al had been transferred the day before. He still hadn't seen or spoken to his father since he'd been brought in with a parade of crowd-control police units and hundreds of avid onlookers with smartphones and press with mics and cameramen.

Al, who was under twenty-four-hour police and nurse supervision, wasn't allowed more than one visitor at a time and was considered high-risk. If his father was as ambitious in ending his life as he'd been in building his life, then the hell for the Franco family wasn't close to being over.

A preliminary mental evaluation had been completed, but there were more extensive follow-ups to come. Alzheimer's hadn't been ruled out, depression had been the preliminary diagnosis and schizophrenic disorders were still possibilities.

Al had admitted to delusions of seeing his deceased first wife, Gloria, had hallucinated her likeness and voice and thought he'd been interacting with her while hiding in Italy. Rescued from some market in Sicily, he'd suffered severe blood loss from slashes to his wrists, and Italian authorities had worked with the hospital to extradite him to the United States immediately after stabilization.

Santino's godfather, Gian DiGorgio, had been arrested on a warrant granted following the authentication of a video recording of Al recanting Gian's involvement in running a criminal gambling ring out of DiGorgio Royal Casino and his arrangement of Alessandro's escape from Nevada.

At five-forty, Santino had another twenty minutes left of his dusk till dawn shift in the waiting room outside the hospital's psychiatric ward. He wondered what difference there was between a privately funded psychiatric ward and any other. Better-tasting coffee, maybe.

Hazarding a cup of brew, he grimaced but drank it down black anyway. Once his brother arrived, he'd need the extra shot of caffeine to calmly wade through the mob outside and drive home to rest. Chances were he wouldn't sleep in the middle of a sunny day, but he'd get himself to relax and try to ease his brain, which was sprinting a constant marathon.

"I held up my end of the bargain."

Santino's hand automatically crushed the empty foam cup he held. Zaf wore a baseball cap and flannel shirt over a black outfit similar to what he'd worn when Santino had met him in February. "What do you want? He's already in police custody."

"I put him in custody, Santino. I found him in Italy and got his confession."

"Then instead of turning him over right off the damn bat, you let him psyche himself until he thought the best way out was to gut his wrists? He almost *died*."

"If he hadn't cut himself, he *would* be dead. His old friend Gian DiGorgio was done following up behind him and wanted him eliminated. Your question's how did I know that, huh? I had Gian watched, too. To get my clean indisputable proof, I put a few of my boys in place in Italy and DiGorgio hired one of them as the doer."

*God.* "How did you get my father to confess?"

"That's where you held up your end of the bargain." Zaf got closer on the pretense of getting a drink of coffee. "Say hi to Bindi Paxton for me."

"That means what?"

"Is her skin as soft as it looks? In another life I might've taken anything a woman threw at me if her skin was soft."

"Son of a bitch."

"Since I'm not playing God, and all the players have free will, I can't say I knew exactly what you'd do. I thought you or she would get the account shut down. I figured you'd get the money, not the panties." Zaf paused, considered. "Yeah, that was crude even for me. But hey, proof of the hooking up is all your father needed to give up coming for her."

"Who took the pictures? Cecelia Whit from the hotel?"

"Cecelia's one of the good ones, and no, it wasn't her. You're off on that. But I don't out my sources, so you're not going to get a nice, clean *Scooby-Doo* mystery tie-up. For now, take comfort in the fact that Alessandro Franco's under medical and police protection, and your godfather's in custody. I say for now because it's not over." Zaf finally took a foam cup and filled it with coffee. "Crap, you'd think these people have enough problems without having to drink bad coffee in a place like this."

As if he'd planned it, the moment Zaf disappeared into a stairwell, security personnel came passing through. A minute later the stairwell door opened again and a guy carrying a box labeled Lost and Found cut through the waiting room. At the top of the heap were a flannel shirt and an Angels baseball cap.

Santino got off his chair and went to the stairwell because he had to, but found no one there and heard no footsteps above or below. Going back to the waiting area, he met up with Nate. "Thanks, man," he said, reluctant to leave this place but resolving to accept that he could share this burden and heartache with his brother.

"Don't come back here until you get some sleep," Nate said grimly. "Charlotte's willing to join the rotation."

"She'd do that, after everything our father did to make hell for her people?"

"She forgives him."

"Maybe it's easier for her," Santino said. "She didn't love him."

"Could be why." Nate clapped his back, and gave him a brotherly push toward the exit. "Remember—sleep first, then get back here."

Santino knew his weariness ran bone-deep, but the coffee made him alert as ever as he took to the road. Concentrating on the road still didn't make him stop thinking about his phone, waiting for the screen to light up with Bindi's name. A call, a text, *anything*. He'd tried to call her yesterday, when he'd been reeling with shock, but it had gone straight to voice mail, and without hearing her voice, he hadn't known what to say.

By now she had to have been clued in that Alessandro was in custody and in Las Vegas. But she hadn't come near the psychiatric ward where he was being held and treated. If he didn't know her the way he'd come to, he would be cynical enough to suspect that she was making money telling her story to the media. But he did know her, knew that she was empathetic and had a heart as vulnerable as anyone else's, if not more so.

And he hoped he hadn't wrecked beyond repair what they'd had together.

Santino didn't call her. He didn't drive to his condo and brainstorm what he could say to persuade her to give him another chance to get it right with her. He drove to East Dune, parked in the lot and went to her door.

Bindi opened the door, leaned against it and blinked slowly at him.

"I called yesterday," he said from the hall, wanting her to speak and give him the comfort of her voice, "about my father. It went straight to voice mail."

"I must've been on the plane. I was in Illinois yesterday, and I saw the report on TV." She allowed him in with a nod and shut the door. "I picked up my keys and bag to go out the door and visit him, but I keep pulling back because I don't know if I belong there anymore. With any of you."

"What he did to you, me, Nate, the Blues and everyone he affected with that gambling scheme—it should be unforgivable. Does it make any of us wrong if we find out we're in a place where forgiveness isn't possible?" It made him jittery to be so close to his father but still be denied the closure he'd crawl across broken glass for.

"Neither of us should make that judgment against someone else, Santino. Forgive or forever blame—it's an individual decision. But I…I went home, well, to the place that used to be my home, and I saw my parents for who they are. They're hard people motivated by something I don't understand, and despite all the ways they hurt me, I went back there willing to forgive because it was my choice to try it."

"Do you forgive them?"

"I can't until they change." Bindi abruptly pressed a fist to her mouth, and he immediately took her in his arms when she started to cry. "Remembering is one thing, but reliving it is—"

He eased her onto the sofa, and her head rested against his shoulder. "What did they do? The pills?"

"No. I guess your informant missed out on the worst two years of my life. When I was eighteen, my daddy started persuading me to 'be friendly' to men who could offer him a political edge. If he gave them me, they'd give him support or would sponsor him or, as of yesterday, head up his presidential campaign." She sniffled. "None of them cared about me, and afterward Daddy always said he loved me right before he told me to go take a shower."

He saw red. "I'm so sorry, Bindi." The words didn't seem enough. If she could bear to take him there so he could put his fist in Roscoe Rayburn Paxton's face, that might be a decent start. "Your parents should've loved you enough to protect you."

"I don't think they can love me. And I don't think I should force them to fake it." She sighed. "When I was twenty, I got away from Illinois. I busted Daddy for cheating. He'd been doing it for years—even during ComicCon. The shirt I love so much? He'd bought it for some D-cup woman he met, and I took it first."

What a hell for a kid to face alone. Santino took her hand. "Why do you keep that shirt?"

"I thought I could pretend we were happy then. We weren't, though, and I didn't get away until I got booted from college for defacing this art project that represented lies. All of these people had written their lies, and I thought I could do it. So I wrote out my lies, then backpedaled and covered the entire thing in black paint."

"And after that—"

"You can figure that out. I got away from my parents so they couldn't hurt me, but then I just hurt myself. Yesterday, I said no and I left them. I forgave myself more than I ever have before yesterday, because it was so damn clear that I'm finally changing. I'm okay with myself. And you—are you're okay with me?"

Santino looked at her. Her tears, her sniffles, the way her mouth wavered because she fought so hard for composure—he loved it all. "I'd have to be, since I'm in love with you."

Her eyes widened. "Santino…I didn't tell you all of this because I'm asking for love donations. We can forget you said it."

"Then I'll just say it again until you can trust that I mean it. I love you, Bindi, and I'm in love with you. This is where I am, wanting you in my life."

With a slow, blinding smile spreading across her face, Bindi stood up and led him to her room. "Show me. I want to know what it's like to be with a man who loves me."

He gently bumped her backward onto the bed and climbed on top. Gently, and then frenzied, they pulled at each other's clothes. He was prepared to stop if her emotions demanded it. She'd made that sacrifice for him, and he accepted that sex between them wouldn't always be fantastic or paradise. Paradise was imperfection. It was sharing a shopping list with somebody and having a good time in a market. It was about laughing and teasing and protection and getting each other.

Never had he had that with Tabitha.

"I want to tell you something," he said, helping her peel off her jeans. "You're beautiful, and for reasons that no one else has been smart enough to see before. You don't believe it and now I understand why."

"I'm trying to see what you see."

"Right now I see a woman who's not gonna get sex this time."

"I'm not?" Bindi started to sit up, and that put her in perfect position to be kissed thoroughly.

"You're going to be made love to."

"Oh. Okay." Searching his eyes, she grabbed his shoulders and held on as he rocked into her with a few deliberate thrusts. Locking together, they moved slowly until sweat coated them both.

He wanted to love her for the rest of their lives. When they came, it left them weak, exhausted and so intoxicated that they lay together on top of the sheets, not exactly sure what had just happened but glad that it had. And it fulfilled them both so unexpectedly that Bindi forgot to run to the shower and Santino forgot that sleep didn't come easy.

It was past midnight when Bindi awoke next to Santino. They got up leisurely, enjoying these quiet minutes in a darkened room, showering together and then dressing to face the outside world together.

They separated outside her building, taking separate vehicles to the same destination. The hospital where Alessandro was under close watch was a striking building gloriously illuminated at night. The landscaping was humble yet creative, and she admired the care taken to the topiaries. Professionals were recruited and trusted to bring this type of artistic blessing to commercial grounds all the time. Maybe one day she could be a professional and share her designs and visions with clients.

Someone—*her* someone—loved her. Anything was possible.

Bindi slipped past the throng of reporters while they were distracted by Santino. Once safely inside, they joined his brother in the psychiatric ward's waiting room. Two chairs were available, and when Santino made his choice, she had the option to step away and stand near the refreshments bar, or sit between the two brothers. One loved her; the other didn't particularly like her.

But that was the thing with families. Not everyone meshed, but somehow you found a way to fit together or you gravitated elsewhere.

Bindi sat on the vacant chair, and out of her periphery, she saw Nate shift his arm to free up the armrest between them. "Thanks," she mumbled, even though the single word felt inadequate. She propped her elbow up and silently sighed, content for this shard of a moment.

"Visitors for Alessandro Franco?"

The three glanced up in unison at a man who introduced himself as Doctor Gomez.

"Are you three his children?"

Santino and Nate looked at her, and she felt her skin flush. "No," she clarified. "They are. But I'm Al's ex-fiancée and I'm in love with his son, Santino. May I visit him anyway?"

Orderlies crossing the space had a hitch in their step as they eavesdropped.

"Uh…" Doctor Gomez stammered. "Yeah. Yes, uh, you may see him."

Bindi got up but first knelt in front of Santino. "I love you. Okay? I don't know if it's a good thing for you, or if staying in Las Vegas is even the best decision for me, or if one of us is going to end up hurt because of it, but I do love you. It just seemed a lot like lying to not tell you."

Before he could comment, she straightened and added, "Come with me to see your father." After a moment, he followed her and the doctor to Al's visitation room. The room was small, but not as sterile as she'd seen on television and in films. The space was simply decorated with neutral tones of paint and windows set high on the walls.

Alessandro sat at a table, his hair a youthful black but his face that of an old and tired man. "Santino," he said, lifting his arms up as if to embrace his son.

"No contact," a stern voice warned. Two uniformed police officers were hovering close and a nurse was stationed at each of the four corners of the visitation room. A high-profile patient who was connected to NFL scandal *and* had given a confession that had landed a ruthless casino owner in custody got the psyche ward star treatment.

"Nate's here, too," Santino said to his father as he and Bindi sat across from Alessandro. "He's waiting outside. Look, your attorneys resigned. You need representation. We—we— Dammit, Dad, we started to think you were dead and then we find out that you tried to kill yourself."

"When it happened, I thought of you and Nate and I wanted to see my boys. It was already done but I wanted to live for you and your brother. Do you…" His voice shook. "Do you hate me?"

Bindi turned slightly toward Santino. What would he say? Hate made severing a complicated relationship easier.

But as always, Santino placed honesty over taking the easy route. "I don't hate you, Dad. You're sick, you need help and you need to answer for the hell you and Gian brought down. But I love you, if that makes a difference."

Alessandro nodded and his mouth stayed shut in a firm line. When he lifted his head as Santino rose from the table to leave the visitation room, his eyes were rimmed in red. "So, Bindi Paxton. If you knew then what you know now, would you have still accepted my ring?"

"What would be the point of answering that, Al?" When he appeared crestfallen, she approached her response from a different angle. "I'm not proud of the reasons why I took your ring, but I'm not sorry I met you. Maybe I shouldn't say this, but because of you I met Santino. I love him. He loves me."

"You're going to take his ring?"

She didn't dare look behind her, but hoped that Santino had already left. "He hasn't offered one. I don't want a diamond. I want more out of a relationship than that. Like a home or a sense of belonging—things like that." Bindi openly studied his thickly bandaged arms, and it hurt her square in the chest to think of him parting flesh and vein and tendons to escape what he'd done. "Al?"

"Yes?"

"It gets better, if you let it. And I forgive you."

When Bindi returned to her seat in the waiting room, she saw Santino walking toward the stairwell with an intimidating goliath of a man. "What's Marshall Blue doing here?" she asked Nate, who remained seated even though Santino had said they had agreed to shifts.

"His exact words were, 'In times of personal crisis, I like to focus on business. Let's talk business. It won't take long,'" Nate relayed, leaning forward to prop his forearms on his thighs. "I was about to go, but I'm staying to find out what the hell he wants."

"Still excited to be marrying into the Blue family?" she murmured discreetly.

"Ask Lottie if she's excited to be marrying into the Franco family. Thing is, I don't think of it that way. I'm marrying Charlotte and only Charlotte."

Bindi smiled and she thought for a flicker of a second that he'd smiled back.

True enough, in a Las Vegas minute Santino was heading back their way.

"What did Marshall want?" his brother asked without preamble.

"To offer me a job. There's a weakness in offensive coordinating. He wants a meeting at the stadium this week. I didn't say yes or no."

Bindi didn't mind that his brother assailed him with hushed questions; she was speechless. Marshall Blue had offered a Franco a job within his franchise? Nate had resigned from his athletic trainer position after his first camp under Blue leadership—but that probably had everything to do with him wanting to keep up a relationship with his colleague Charlotte.

What kind of business strategy were the Blues trying to put into place?

Bindi didn't ignore the thought that if Santino accepted the position, he'd be staying in Las Vegas. As for her, she couldn't go home again, as her friend Toya had, but could she stay in this city where she had no chance of being constantly reminded of her past mistakes?

Could she really walk away from the man she loved, even if it allowed her to walk away from her old self?

Alessandro missed Gloria. He missed the moments in which he could be certain she was near, could hear her voice and know that he was loved. The love of a patient and tough woman was a miracle amongst life's tragedies.

Yet he didn't miss the consequences of being visited by his wife. Today he'd seen his sons, and though their heartbreak was still evident on their stoic faces, he was at peace beyond the deep throbbing pain in his wounds.

"One more visitor," a guard told him when he started to push back from the table.

Settling back in the seat, he froze as Marshall Blue was escorted into the room. Marshall, with his coffee-colored skin and hard, angry expression, was a giant in size and power, who could pulverize with his fists or with a business move—Al had realized that. Still, he'd crafted lies against the man out of desperation.

Why weren't the guards protecting him? Why had they allowed Marshall to enter this room, when the papers and internet were chock-full of the details of bad blood between them? Why did everyone want to see him hurt, when losing his wife had hurt worse than any physical pain could?

"Guard, you want to escort him out?" Al demanded when Marshall was next to the table. "Guard!"

"Calm down, Alessandro Franco," Marshall Blue said, as if he had all of eternity to do what he'd come here to do. "I'm not here to harm you. You're under protection."

"I don't trust you."

"Wise man. You're not all gone up here." Marshall tapped his temple. "I have something for you. It's a privilege, and I'll be taking it back when I leave. We're just going to have a conversation now."

Warily, Alessandro sat silent as Marshall smoothed his custom designer suit down the front, unbuttoned the jacket and sat down opposite him. On the table he set down a brand-new pack of playing cards.

Alessandro sighed weakly. Opening the box would aggravate his wounds. The pain medication was beginning to lose its potency. "Cards?"

"I'll open them. I can shuffle them if you can't."

Alessandro moistened his lips. They'd become so dry and cracked in Sicily. He waited for Marshall Blue to clear the stack of the box, and then he set them facedown on the table. "Simple game today, Alessandro. War."

"Okay." Alessandro shuffled despite the ache in his fresh wounds. The crisp cards fell into formation magnificently. "And what is it that you have to tell me while we play?"

"I've offered your son Santino a job on my team. Offensive coordinator position. His stats are impeccable, and I received some privileged information that he had been in training for a year to return to the field in a jersey. It's not going to happen for him, though. If he didn't already tell you, let him do it in his own time. But I want you to know that I am looking out for your boys."

"What about Nate?"

"Nate is engaged to my daughter, Charlotte."

"*Bella* Charlotte." Alessandro shook his head, bewildered. He was missing everything, and for what?

"When he marries my daughter, he'll become part of my family whether he accepts that or not. I'll watch out for your children, Alessandro. That is something you can trust."

Alessandro began to deal the cards, slowly, solemnly. "Why help me?"

"I have a wife that I love."

"My wife. My Gloria…"

Marshall nodded slightly as Alessandro continued to deal. "Tell me about your wife."

# Chapter 12

Bindi didn't find herself sitting at the rear of a synagogue because she had made a firm life-directing decision. She was here for quiet and to better remember her maternal grandmother, who'd asked her to consider remembering all the facets of her that made her an individual—that made her Bindi Paxton.

She was Christian, Jewish, African-American, German, Polish, Armenian, Native American—and yet she was none of those things, living disconnected from everything that made her Bindi Paxton. The pressure to choose, to settle on an alliance, was one she resisted. All or none was the choice she'd given herself when she'd left her parents' home ten years ago.

Today, she wondered if any religion would have her and all the issues she came with. Sitting with her black lace-gloved hands folded in her lap and the lace trim of her scarf tickling the sides of her face, she sat quietly and wondered if the rabbi would notice her.

"Have you come to pray?" he asked before she realized that he watched her with a peaceful curiosity.

Bindi shook her head. "I'm not a member."

"Are you Jewish?"

"I don't know," she said, and expected irritation.

But the rabbi only nodded.

"Rabbi?"

"Yes?"

"I don't know much about religion, but my heritage is complicated and part of my family practices Christianity while another part practices Judaism. I don't want to choose, but…I want to belong to somebody—to something."

"Hybrid religious identities are becoming more common," the rabbi shared, moving so slowly his robes barely rustled. "We will welcome and accept you should you choose Judaism or a hybrid religious identity. Please don't take the decision lightly. Why is it so important to you? I'd like to hear your answer to that."

"Because…" Well, *why* was it? "Because I don't belong anywhere. I belong to me…and I'm important."

"Who says you're important?"

"I do. I love myself."

Smiling, the rabbi nodded.

"May I sit here for a few more minutes?" Bindi asked, smiling, too.

"Of course."

Bindi wasn't waiting for anything, just sitting still and listening to nothing. Who she would be and where she would go was truly a decision that only she could make. The reality of it made her feel alone yet brave.

There was that, too. Bindi Paxton was brave.

It was raining when Bindi turned away from her windowsill plants and called Santino's phone. When he answered, she blurted, "I love you."

"I love you," he said. "I think we should start all of our phone calls off like that."

"I want to see you. Are you home?"

"I'm going to be someplace else, actually. Write this address down?"

Bindi jotted it on a grocery list pad and rushed through her apartment to dress up her button-down shirt and sexy jeans with tall brown boots, a hunter-green jacket and tons of mismatched beaded bracelets. Rainy days were excellent days to make life-sculpting decisions.

They were also terrible days to leave the house without any hair coverage other than a glossy magazine. She stopped in front of a stone-fronted house that looked like it might belong to a wealthy fairy-tale giant that knew zilch about landscaping.

Getting out of the Grand Cherokee, she walked around the front of the vehicle, holding the magazine in place on top of her head. As she neared the veranda, her jacket began to feel heavy from all the absorbed rainwater.

Santino, way too sexy for a rainy day in a dark gray suit and white shirt, opened the door before she made it up the steps. Instead of letting her in, he joined her outside and took her free hand. "This way."

"This feels a little covert. Whose house is this? Is this what you experienced when I asked you to bring a car seat to my apartment?"

"First, what do you think of all these hedges and shrubs and trees?"

"They have potential," she said slowly. "A little TLC from somebody with an eye for it, and repairing the entire law isn't insurmountable."

"How much time do you think that'd take?"

"A bit. This property is…wow. The grounds are all the privacy anyone could want in this part of Las Vegas." Now the rain was stroking into her hair in spite of her efforts to shield it. She lowered the magazine. "So whose property?"

"Mine."

"You own this house? Why did you buy it?"

"So my someone could have somewhere to belong."

Bindi laughed, or was it a cry? She didn't know if the wetness on her face was from the rain or her tears, but she didn't care as she grabbed his face and kissed him. "You know what *someone* and *somewhere* mean?"

"I picked up on them when you and your friend referenced them."

"And you bought a place that I could belong to? But Las Vegas…"

"If you don't want Las Vegas, you don't have to have it. Your future is your choice. But I'm here to tell you that this house will be here. And I want you here. With me. Because I love you, and no, I don't want you to run away from Las Vegas and what you did wrong. Leaving a place doesn't mean you can escape what you're running from. My father tried that."

Bindi dropped her forehead to his chest. He raised a couple of damn good points. Running wouldn't guarantee that she could forget who she used to be. Still, she was free to do as she pleased.

"Fight for happiness. Fight for this—you and me."

They were a *this* now. And he was her someone. He was already fighting to keep her in his life because he loved her. Sometimes love meant letting go. But other times, like right now, it meant trusting someone to protect you.

"What's inside the house right now?" she asked, looking up at him.

"A baby grand piano and a box of random novelty stuff."

"You rescued them!" Just like he rescued her, and let her rescue him.

"If you want, I can teach you to play."

"So you'll teach me piano and I can teach you how to conquer this landscaping dilemma? The only other thing I can offer you is love."

"Love?"

She nodded. "That's all."

"That's everything, Bindi."

Bindi looked from him to the massive house. No, home. Their home. With massive, sturdy trees that'd make perfect structures to choose for a swing. If not for a child someday, then for her. "Take me home."

Kissing her, he took her hand and they raced through the rain to get cracking on their future.

\* \* \* \* \*

They're turning
up the heat!

# BET ON
## *My*
# HEART

## *J.M. Jeffries*

Donovan Russell is trading his five-star Parisian kitchen for the
restaurants at his grandmother's Reno casino. Now he just needs his
new pastry chef to follow his rules! Because where Donovan is all
structure and precision, Hendrix Beausolies cooks with instinct and
experimentation. But when someone starts sabotaging their kitchens,
they may discover a shared passion for more than just food...

### PASSION'S GAMBLE

*Available April 2015!*

www.Harlequin.com

KPJMJ3980415

# REQUEST YOUR FREE BOOKS!

## 2 FREE NOVELS
## PLUS 2 FREE GIFTS!

**KIMANI™ ROMANCE**

### Love's ultimate destination!